Niall Stewart was born in 1982 and lives with his fiancé in London. *The Beautiful Anatomy of Despair* is his first novel.

For my aunt, Susan Stewart.
1943–2020

Niall Stewart

THE BEAUTIFUL
ANATOMY OF DESPAIR

AUSTIN MACAULEY PUBLISHERS™

LONDON • CAMBRIDGE • NEW YORK • SHARJAH

A CIP catalogue record for this title is available from the British Library.

ISBN 9781398402133 (Paperback)
ISBN 9781398402140 (Hardback)
ISBN 9781398402157 (ePub e-book)

www.austinmacauley.com

First Published 2022
Austin Macauley Publishers Ltd®
1 Canada Square
Canary Wharf
London
E14 5AA

Table of Contents

"Last night in the warm spring air while I was blazing my tirade against someone who doesn't interest me, it was love for you that set me afire."

Frank O'Hara

| PART ONE |
KNOWING ME, KNOWING YOU

2014

TRISTAN

The Aristotelian path to happiness is surely a treacherous one, demanding our excellence and virtue at every step. What can we learn, really, from people who were resolute it is not the purpose of life to be happy? What, really, is the point of well-being if it does not contain at least occasional pleasure? Are we to be dismissed as hedonists because it is better when the pleasant outweighs the painful?

We are wired to seek out happiness; it guarantees us some sort of future, and we are condemned to pursue it forever.

*

Tristan opened his eyes and surveyed the wigwam roof of the six-sided room as sunshine gushed through the floor to ceiling windows, adorning everyone he could see with a springtime honeyed glow.

San Francisco, day six. He was sitting cross-legged on the floor trying to meditate, encouraging his mind to wander around the circumference of its consciousness, but the task was deeply uncomfortable, and taxing in the most unsettling of ways.

He looked at the contours of Seb's sun-kissed neck, at his sacrosanct sheen. Tristan knew nothing about him, not even the sound of his voice.

We are at the mercy of our desires, constrained by their relentlessness. What little strength we have to assert ourselves over them.

Tristan paid Seb attention simply for the thrill of seeing him, the euphoria of keeping him just in view.

We know so little about what we want, other than the knowledge we want it. The picture in our mind is rarely accurate; we pin our hopes on the most fleeting of objectives. Who are we, really, if our dreams are always beyond our experience?

The days passed, and Tristan found comfort in routine: five am starts and pre-breakfast yoga, his woodland walks, the dharma training teaching him to move into the quiet of his mind. He stopped shaving, hoping his stubble might grow into the hint of a beard.

"I didn't like you at first," Seb would tell him years later.

How terrible it is, the power we freely give to others, the meanings we attach to nothing very much at all.

Day nine. The group gathered, and the microphone made its way round the circle. A girl in her late twenties wearing a pink beanie performed a rap; a man with a beard and a gut tried to start a panel discussion; someone spoke of winding down their business, giving all their possessions to charity, finding a new path.

Tristan made his way through the suitcases and jackets as Seb observed from under the chestnut tree, looking like someone to whom the rules didn't apply. Tristan froze, electrified; his composure dissolved at the sight of him.

"Are they good?" Tristan asked of the freshly baked goods clutched in Seb's left hand.

"Really good." He spoke with a mid-Atlantic inflection, his posture holding the world at a distance.

"I'm gonna head in and grab one," said Tristan, his first ever use of 'gonna'. Seb waved him the smallest of goodbyes as he scraped the embers of his Lucky Strike along the bark.

Inside, Tristan poured ginger tea into a mug, took one of the treats from the tray and stood in the centre of the room. He spotted the spindly woman with the kind eyes and the bearded man in his late forties grateful for any attention Tristan gave him, which hadn't been much. Their eyes met—a social carelessness—and he approached to applaud Tristan for his effort; the retreat's only Brit. It was a detail Tristan regretted sharing at the introductory session, volunteering his outsider status.

"Thank you," Tristan replied, still struggling with West Coast assertiveness, all equivocation absent.

"You know," the man continued, "I thought you might be Swedish."

Tristan looked at him quizzically.

"Your *Björn Borg* underwear?"

"Oh."

He couldn't have seen more than the waistband, Tristan realised, but he disliked hyper-sexualised talk; it was cliché and it made him uncomfortable, and he wanted to shut it down. He saw Seb circulating at the other side of the room, offering a replenished tray to passers-by, people converging on him.

"But I suppose you being British makes sense," the man continued, oblivious. "You scoop peas onto your fork like grandma would."

Tristan was perturbed by the admission of covert scrutiny. "I didn't realise the Brits had a monopoly on that. Or grandmothers, come to think of it."

What an awkward dance it all is. How oblivious we are to the fictions which stand between us.

"Let's join the others," Tristan insisted, and started walking towards the quickly expanding circle before the man could object. He squeezed himself between Seb and a woman who later told them they looked like brothers. Some of the group discussed whether to keep in touch; with a disconcerting casualness, those who'd tried before said not to bother.

Seb tucked his thumbs into the sleeves of his hoodie and looked at Tristan: "We should hang out." He took him aside, tore off a piece of paper pinned to the noticeboard and scrawled his number in curly handwriting too big for the page. He displayed a confidence so brazen Tristan felt shamed by comparison.

*

Tristan was standing at the entrance to the retreat waiting for a cab. He hadn't pre-booked and the chances of one turning up any time soon seemed remote. Someone leaving the retreat in a small Volkswagen offered him a ride downtown, which he accepted. They talked about meditation methodology; Tristan pretended to know more than he did, and she did a good job of pretending not to notice. He asked her to deposit him on a side street off Castro. He chose it at random; he had nowhere he needed to be. But he acclimatised, found a guesthouse which could accommodate him, deposited his inappropriately large suitcase at its reception and relocated to a nearby tea lounge to log his thoughts, where the blend he chose at random was dispatched in a test tube filled with luminous green liquid. He sipped at it tentatively, enjoying the way it looked more than the way it tasted, and wrote three turgid paragraphs before setting the paper to one side and screwing the cap back onto the barrel of his fountain pen.

Tristan spent the next three days walking the streets, checking in and out of hotels and trying out different parts of the city, visiting SOMA and the planetarium, dining alone, avoiding pick-up artists in the *End-Up*. He walked along Ocean Beach with a high street shoulder bag someone mistook for Moroccan market bespoke. They told him through the mist they liked his style and Tristan could feel his walk becoming a swagger.

Tristan assessed the contents of his suitcase, looking for something to wear which was clean and uncreased; his stock was depleted, and the polo shirt he chose smelled of damp. He left his hotel in plenty of time, intent on arriving in control of himself and resplendent, but, refusing to activate data roaming, he lost his way twice and arrived with only minutes to spare, glossed in sweat. His eyes darting around the room; he recognised no one.

He selected a section of floor with the middle dug out to make room for legs and lowered himself onto one of the cushions.

Seb arrived just after eleven, wearing jeans and colourful canvas shoes and an oversized, slightly crushed, white T-shirt, over which he exerted more control than it did over him.

"Nice table," said Seb, as he lowered himself onto the floor and tucked in his legs. His smile made Tristan self-conscious about his teeth.

"Yeah. I hope you weren't hoping to be comfortable."

"It's fine. It reminds me of the meditation hall."

"I can see that," Tristan agreed.

Seb looked at the coffee machine as it hissed at customers queuing at the counter; clouds of steam enveloping the spotlights hanging from the ceiling, a bohemia managed with ruthless precision.

"What's this?" Seb asked, pointing at the Japanese teapot and the neon orange concoction in the cup next to it, placing both of his hands on the opposite side of the table as he did so. Claiming all of it for himself, Tristan wondered, or an initiation of intimacy?

"Sobacha. Notes of buckwheat, popcorn and straw."

Seb rolled his eyes. "I'll just have Chai."

He summoned a server and placed his order.

"So," Tristan began, "I didn't think you'd come."

"You were wrong."

*

The following evening, Tristan arrived at the house which Seb's parents had recently taken on as a long-term let, the residence of Professor and Mrs. Self. Wearing a purple velvet jacket and regretting his decision not to wear a tie, he knocked on the door and the man who opened it ushered him into a blue and gold reception room redolent of Oval Office colours. He accepted a saucer of champagne and sipped at it as he searched for Seb, trying to hover on the fringes and listen into other people's conversations, but his youth marked him out as conspicuous and people wanted to include him. They called him young man and asked what he did. Tristan tried out a variety of answers, figuring out which pose to adopt, which mask was the best fit. Some seemed genuinely interested; that their approbation was so easy to obtain made him like them a little bit less.

Tristan hated socialising; he always felt the need to show off.

"He's upstairs if you're wondering," She didn't need to say who she was. Tristan figured it out as soon as he turned around and saw her face.

*

Seb was twenty and Camilla almost ten years his senior and, given that the not quite a decade gap seemed to explain their particular brand of sibling dynamic, their parents sometimes wished they had been more careful.

For many years, Camilla took great pleasure in telling Seb she had ten years on him and he should act accordingly. This led to an uneasy standoff, but she was persistent, and it did yield some results: in the early years, it meant she would be Batman and he would be Robin, it meant she always got to be Yoshi when they played *Mario Kart*, and it meant all the teachers knew they were siblings because they routinely ignored each other at school. But as the years wore on, she had come to see Seb less as her younger brother and more simply as her brother, someone on whom she could rely, someone who knew her past because it was his past too, an anchor point in a world which seemed increasingly fleeting.

Three hours before the guests were scheduled to arrive, Seb picked up a light blue shirt with one finger and eyed it with disgust.

"Is this some kind of fucking joke?" Seb asked his mother.

"Language," she replied, her focus elsewhere.

There was an inch-long crease underneath the left-side pocket, but that wasn't the problem. The problem was the shirt felt slightly too short in the arms and when he pulled back his shoulders, the material around the third button pulled tight.

"I mean, look at this!" He was still looking at the shirt, it was still hanging off his finger, it was still slightly creased, and his mother still wasn't looking.

"Do you know anything about this?" he asked Camilla.

"You're asking me if I know anything about a shirt which the laundry service ironed for you? The answer to your question would be no."

She fixed her eyes on him and saw Seb struggling to conceal his anger, so she wasn't particularly surprised when he started screaming at her, calling her all sorts, but when he pounced forward looking a bit deranged, that did catch her off-guard, and when she stepped back, she stumbled, and they fell onto the tiled floor. But she flipped him round, got him by the ears and told him he was her little elf and when Seb told her to let go, she knew she had won.

"You really are a terrible misogynist," she told him, his ears still in her hands.

"It's not misogyny," he replied. "It's you."

Their mother told them they were as bad as each other.

"She started it," Seb replied, the instant gratification of blaming somebody else.

"And stop saying 'fuck'."

"You say 'fuck' all the time."

"That is not the point."

It was exchanges like these which confirmed to Camilla Seb's favoured status. It caused her pain: it was like fighting for supremacy with a myth, saddled with all the responsibility but none of the power.

When Seb returned to the pile of shirts, Camilla suggested he wear the gingham, but she knew he wouldn't because the cotton wasn't two-ply, and the collar wasn't button-down.

*

Camilla took Tristan by the arm and led him into the dining room.

20

"I've not checked where I'm sitting," Tristan told her.

"Don't worry. Follow my lead."

She showed him where to sit and, taking her place next to him, he pressed into the button-tufted backrest and inspected the place card, his name embossed in gold calligraphy. He counted twenty-six chairs, tried unsuccessfully to cross his legs—either the table was too low, or the seat of his chair was too high—and allowed himself to register his growing unease.

"I'm not sure I should stay," he whispered to Camilla.

She placed her hand on his thigh. Her pinkie almost touched his penis.

"Oh, don't stay for him," she said, not matching his whisper. "But you'll stay for me."

A waiter sloshed some wine into his glass, and he gulped it down. All but one of the chairs was occupied but the room was quiet; its formality and scale bringing out people's inhibitions. Camilla told him the chair immediately opposite them was for Seb. The pulse of excitement he felt even at the mention of his name.

"Is he coming?"

"Not if something better comes up, no."

Tristan envied her access to the less glossy version of him, to the Seb as he imagined it who played video games in his pants.

Professor Self sat at the head of the table. A man whispered into his ear, looking flustered.

"That's about the photographer," Camilla told Tristan. "It's very important to my father these events are properly documented."

"Does anyone actually look at the photographs?" Tristan asked.

"Not to my knowledge."

Tristan told her he preferred his photography staged; only a pose captured what someone would rather not reveal.

Camilla's father welcomed the assembled guests, making eye contact with a chosen few. The staff served the starters and Camilla started talking to the man sitting on her right, leaving Tristan to fork at his pear and gorgonzola salad alone. He picked around the walnuts. As the plates were cleared, Professor Self instigated a discussion which enveloped a slowly widening circle of people. He sought out their view, called them by their name, adding one or two others every three or four minutes. Tristan looked at his empty wine glass and glanced at Camilla. She seemed relaxed, too familiar with the developing spectacle to care, as a woman whose face looked like a Mariah Carey lyric talked about her hard-working husband.

*

"I'm sorry about that," Seb told him afterwards.

"It's fine. It was unexpected, is all," Tristan replied, giving his love for free.

"No, it was painful. I feel bad."

The ease with which Seb apologised caused a flash of recognition: this boy would tear him limb from limb, yet Tristan found himself unable to resist reaching out to touch his face.

TOBY

The Epicurean ideal imagines a soul absent of all pain, freedom from all worry, an unquantifiable bliss in which no desire goes unfulfilled. What a pitiful form of ecstasy, banishing pain forevermore!

How can we know the value of anything without first taking measure of its opposite?

*

Toby was sitting at his desk, wondering if his face had returned to its normal buttery colour. His cheeks still felt hot.

"It's been a while since we had one like that," Rosalind said of the afternoon meeting as she typed this month's password into her computer. Toby and Rosalind had shared an office and the occasional intimate detail for more years than they cared to remember, but it was as much an alliance as it was a friendship; a support network borne out of proximity.

"I don't see the point of him undermining me in front of the team," said Toby, hearing the strain in his voice. In meetings, people noticed his prominent Adam's apple bouncing up and down as he gulped down his words.

Rosalind smiled tolerantly. "At least he knows who you are," she told him. "Usually, he doesn't even remember our names."

"He called me Ben yesterday."

"Oh, that's a compliment. Ben's much better looking."
Deep down, Rosalind rather admired the man and the
management style, but Toby wasn't so sure: he seemed the type
who'd murder the family and burn down the house if life didn't
go his way.

At nine o'clock, Toby waved as casual a goodbye as he could
muster in Rosalind's direction, being careful not to look her in
the eye, and with a quick glance left and right before opening his
office door, he strode into the corridor and made for the fire
escape. He walked across London Bridge elbow to elbow with
the other office workers, headphones in, trainers on, and stood
next to the bollards on the other side of the river as people
funnelled through the gaps, eyes down.

Igor, on time for once, swerved his vehicle over the central
reservation and into the path of a bus. The driver sounded his
horn; Igor returned the compliment, then pressed the buttons
around him at random until the doors unlocked with a muted
clunk. Toby clambered in and they sped off, stopping a few
metres on, the traffic lights at red.

"What?" Igor asked.

"I'm just wondering what happened in your childhood that
made you like this."

The traffic was at a standstill, but Igor seemed not to care,
tapping the steering wheel absent-mindedly to a beat only he
could hear. Toby removed his tie and placed it in the glove
compartment. He was wearing one of his expensive navy suits
but around Igor he felt awkward and out of place, hemmed in
by the wrong type of cloth.

"Is Tristan coming?" Toby asked.

"Unlikely, considering."

"Considering what?"

"He hasn't told you, then?"

"Obviously not."

By the time they reached Notting Hill, it was dark, and all Toby could see was the opaque light from the chandeliers of the white pillared townhouses.

"What is this place?" Toby asked as they approached the restaurant. Its exterior was grey, no signage.

"It's the sort of place where people try to have sex with you in the toilets." Igor liked it because he was on first name terms with the owners and Toby would come to love it because that meant export strength gin martinis. He ordered two, intent on drinking them in quick succession. Igor didn't care.

"Get sloppy drunk if you have to," he told him.

They were seated at the bar on uncomfortably upright chairs. Toby crossed his legs, then heard his father's voice telling him not to. He felt his first greedy gulp of the martini burning its way down his gullet and he swallowed a second gulp which was larger than the first and then a third which was larger still. By the end of the night, the martinis would taste like water.

Igor scrolled through his phone. When he stumbled across something which amused him, he passed it to Toby to corroborate its value. Toby feigned interest, feeling self-consciously pale next to Igor's bronzed sheen, his hair flat and limp.

They were shown to their table. It was a good one, close enough to the action for Igor, far enough away from it for Toby. Igor selected the seat which placed his good ear towards Toby; not that he told anyone and not that anyone would have known, and Toby, who all these years had been pretending not to notice, took the other seat without comment.

They ordered white Rioja without consulting the wine list. It arrived quickly and Toby felt calmer now a bottle of wine and a deliberately oversized beaker from which to drink it were within easy reach. He drained the contents of his martini glass.

Must his life always be an exercise in diminishing returns, dreading the passing of another year, comparing himself to the success of others, telling himself how poor he was, how expensive everything was, why it was easier for those who came before?

As they ate, Toby allowed his eyes to roam the room, in awe of people living their lives.

*

It was midnight and the dull thud of bass pulsed through the steps as they made their way to the entrance on the first floor. An ostentatiously slim man answered the door. He greeted Igor warmly, a kiss on both cheeks. Igor left Toby to struggle with his shoelaces. Igor usually did this; he brought you along only to toss you aside, but that's how you knew he valued you as a friend.

Toby took the cuff links out of his shirt, rolled up his sleeves and looked for somewhere to leave his satchel.

"People are in there," he was told as he approached the nearest door. The young man's tone was friendly; it was offered as advice, though this Toby missed, instinctively offended when told what to do. Toby could be judgemental when it came to first impressions. He saw only what he assumed was there and it meant he was always playing catch-up.

"I just need somewhere to—." Toby trailed off, pointing at his satchel. "I thought it was a bedroom."

"Oh, it is."

Toby felt the need to justify his presence. "I'm here with Igor."

"I see. He bought you dinner then ditched you at a party?"

"We're friends actually."

"You don't look like Igor's friend."

"Isn't that often the way with friendship?" Toby replied.

Toby abandoned his satchel at the front door, expecting never to see it again, as they approached a black marble kitchen counter, a well-stocked bar laid out on it. He wanted a healthy glass of red but none of the wine bottles were open and he didn't trust his shaking hands to use the corkscrew.

"You really don't remember?"

Toby shook his head, too tired to be embarrassed or to continue speaking. "You tried to get with me at that party." Dominick rubbed the right side of his neck as he spoke, working out a knot.

Toby played for time and gave him a flash of recognition that was false. He should have asked which party, and when, but he could feel the gaze of others and decided it was better to be polite.

"That doesn't sound like me," he said eventually. "I'm quite shy."

Dominick didn't believe Toby didn't remember him. But he thought he was interesting, and he thought he was being teased.

"This place is full of fuckboys," Dominick observed of their surroundings. "Their shine wears off, after a while."

"Why are you here then?"

"I don't have anywhere else I need to be."

Toby asked the same question of himself. He wasn't twenty-one anymore, nor did he particularly want to be again; once had been more than enough. He surveyed the scene of beanpole thin, chiselled cheek-boned boys, and felt flat. Was it too late to pretend to be somebody else?

Toby awoke in familiar but unexpected surroundings. It was first light, 06:05 according to the alarm clock on the sleek bedside table beside him, his head was throbbing, and his mouth was dry. Igor was lying next to him, still asleep. Toby forced himself out of bed and made his way into the bathroom, trying to remember what he had said when and to whom. He turned on the shower, averting his gaze from his reflection in the floor to ceiling mirror Igor installed last year, and placed himself under the jet stream of water. He let it hammer onto his skull as he thought of the day which awaited him. As he rubbed shower gel into the skin on his stomach, he looked down at his raggedy circumcision scar and noticed he was losing weight, his muscle tissue losing faith in him as a long-term prospect. He could see his rib cage poking out. He made it to the sink just in time to be sick into it. Igor seemed oblivious, good at sleeping when it didn't suit him to be awake.

He opened Igor's wardrobe. Its five carcasses contained stacks of jeans, cashmere knits and T-shirts arranged by colour. The suits were at the far end, seven or so, all notch lapelled, all navy or grey. Toby chose the one he had seen Igor wear most recently and selected a slim fit business shirt which looked like it had never been worn. He glanced over his shoulder to monitor Igor's movements, but his eyes remained closed. Toby dressed. The fit of the suit was good, but his skin was still moist, sweating out the excesses of the night before. He found and spat on his shoes, buffed them with the towel he had used to shower, located his Blackberry and kissed Igor on the forehead before quietly closing the door behind him.

The Central line at this time of the morning was borderline pleasant and he scrolled through last night's emails to pass the time; there were eighty-three, landing throughout the night from various time zones. Toby tried to assess which ones to read first but only one really grabbed his attention. It was from Dominick Brown, sent at 03:42 and contained no text.

Toby arrived at Chancery Lane shortly before 07:30 and was at his desk fifteen minutes later. One of the nightshift secretaries said good morning.

"Is it?" he replied.

As soon as he sat down, his phone rang. The voice at the other end of the line asked him where he had been.

The day passed. Toby was still on his office phone, had been for the past three hours, and she was talking still. Toby listened with as much interest as he could muster but eventually he put the volume to one bar above zero and hit mute. Still, she continued, raging a paranoid misanthropy. He counted the minutes.

That night, after another fourteen-hour day, he returned home in high spirits, looking forward to the sort of unrestrained drinking he couldn't get away with in public. It gave him easy access to his self-hatred.

When Toby reached the entrance to his block, he stood outside, stranded as he searched his pockets for the plastic key fob to deactivate the lock. He found a fob, but not the fob he needed, and the red light blinked, refusing him entry. The concierge opened the door anyway.

"Everything alright, sir?"

"Can't complain."

Toby had moved five times in two years, each place a smaller version of the one before, each place full of furniture that wasn't his.

As he made his approach down the featureless hallway, he saw his front door was open. It was possible it had been open all this time, that he had simply walked out of his apartment, past caring whether the door closed behind him, past caring whether his possessions were protected. He tried to remember if he had made the decision to do that.

He was worthless, he didn't deserve to own beautiful things. He felt overwhelmed by the impulse to destroy everything in sight.

He brought his injured right hand to eye level and stared at it, trying to focus his vision. It was a deep cut across the fleshy middle rump and the blood erupting from it was luminous and urgent. He made no effort to stem the bleeding.

Toby tore at the nape of his polo shirt—the material ripped quite cleanly—got down on his knees and started dragging himself through the glass.

By the time he was done, all the pictures were off the walls, there were gashes in the plaster at the points of impact, the kitchen cupboards were open, their contents tipped out. He was covered in cuts, and he had scratched out his face on all the photos he could find. He couldn't bear to look at himself for a second longer: the bad skin, the wonky collars, the narrow shoulders of a girl. He looked at the bottle of bleach underneath the sink and had the feeling he was hovering above himself.

As he flailed around on the floor and in the glass, it didn't feel like he had much of a choice. It didn't even feel like he was following through on a choice he now no longer remembered having made. It felt more like the abandonment of choice.

FREDDIE AND CORDELIA

Despite our flaws and our vulnerabilities, despite the dispositions of who we are, we are told the reality of happiness remains forever in our grasp. Is it not the most cynical of all the lies?

At what point is it acceptable to admit we are tiring of the hunt, and losing sight of what we wanted to achieve in the first place, searching in the wrong place for the wrong thing, devoted to the wrong cause, lost but thinking we are found?

What happened to the consolation of transcendent truth, hovering above the squalor of all our understandings?

*

Cordelia asked the waitress if the heater was on.

"It's on."

"It's just it's quite cold."

"The sun's coming out tomorrow. That should help."

"The air around my face is OK, but it's really cold around my legs," Cordelia replied, pointing for emphasis.

Freddie looked at the menu and wondered whether Cordelia, sitting opposite him and who appeared in this lighting to have applied insufficient lotion to withstand the vicissitudes of the Italian sun, could be persuaded into the eight courses. It seemed unlikely; two of them featured mushrooms, and they both were finding it ever harder to maintain their athletic physique.

Twenty minutes in and they had barely spoken, but it was the fourth day of their trip, and they had spent almost no time apart. On arrival at the hotel restaurant, they had each ordered a drink (Negroni for Freddie; Vodka Gimlet for Cordelia) and now they were quietly making their way through these as they monitored the other diners and exchanged knowing looks. Cordelia sipped at hers: part of her had never shaken off her mother's view of women who drink.

They were an attractive couple, oblivious to the attention they periodically received from the mostly older guests who looked at them fondly, remembering, Freddie assumed, past days. Cordelia looked especially poised. When she turned to the barely visible coastline, Freddie seized his chance to stare at the outline of her breasts through the white muslin dress which blended her into the tablecloth.

Cordelia could feel Freddie's gaze. Increasingly, all these resorts looked so similar, she had to remind herself which country she was in.

They worked their way through the courses with a grim determination. The food was good, but the ventilation systems which kept the rooms too hot or too cold had dried out their appetite. They decided against cheese, and the just set buttermilk panna cotta Cordelia put to one side as Freddie slurped at his noisily, drunk.

Committing herself to Freddie, she was reconciled to it, at times she even felt at peace with the decision she made all those years ago. He was her opposite in so many ways, and she envied the simplicity of his outlook, the ambitious and clever middle-class boy who had been told he could do anything, and who worked hard enough and was clever enough to turn that belief into reality, and who now had enough money and status and achievement to his name to be satisfied his approach had been right all along and that it was the model by which everyone else should live, too. Cordelia didn't subscribe to the set of rules which gave order to his life, nor he to hers. They were, to each other, an access point into another way of living. It was a demonstration of their love, because being with each other made life more difficult.

It was a humid evening, the air sticky, and Cordelia felt a thin gloss of sweat form on her skin as they entered their room. Freddie placed his hands on her hips and turned her to face him, peeling off her dress, pressed her against the wall. The scent she was wearing reminded him of gingerbread. She stopped him and walked to the bathroom, leaving the door open behind her. In past days, an invitation, but tonight, not, and by the time she flossed and brushed, Freddie was in bed and had turned off all the lights.

She woke early, crept around the room assembling herself, and made her way to a table set for two on the edge of the hillside looking out at the sea, wearing oversized sunglasses which made her look like a bug.

She scrolled through social media absent-mindedly, awaiting her poached eggs. She rarely contributed, and the only people who posted to her feeds were those with whom she no longer had much contact. She noted another wedding to which she would have expected an invite. When she removed her white cardigan, risking the pale white skin on the top of her arms to the glare of the sun, someone in staff briskly folded it and deposited it onto a tiny ottoman.

The hum of the breakfast service; most of the tables were occupied by people who looked like her parents, or at least who looked like her parents as they were a week ago.

"What you'll understand one day when you have lived as long as we have is that sometimes these things just happen," her father told her. He'd said it with his professional mode activated; that polished, apparently unflappable manner he had spent a lifetime perfecting in the consulting room.

"This feels like being thrown out of my childhood," she told them.

"Well, you are twenty-nine. It was probably time," he replied, patiently.

"And what about you?" she asked, looking at her mother. "Do you have anything to say about this?"

Her mother shook her head. She had no words. The news had made her mute.

*

Mothers liked Freddie; he was the sort of twenty-something they wanted for their daughters, failing whom for themselves, sometimes not so secretly. He was the shape for which high street stores catered and about whom *GQ* wrote. Muscular, but not a muscle man, he didn't understand the retaliation against the mainstream because the mainstream had always worked for him. He liked his life and didn't see what the fuss was about when people said they didn't like theirs. He was as intelligent as they come, in a mainstream sort of way. His only blemish was a scar on his forehead, a war wound from his childhood when he fell out of the treehouse on the family farm, but he no longer saw it when he looked at himself in the mirror, and he'd never once thought about it after the cut stopped bleeding and healed over.

Yet, for all of that, he was a kamikaze: when you were fighting about nothing, he would lob a grenade that was as well past its sell by date as it was specific, and so it turned out he'd been harbouring this or that grudge for years. People wondered where he had the energy to keep all his resentments festering.

"Sometimes, when you make a point," he told Cordelia during their final dinner of the holiday, "you say it with a knuckly hardness which makes you difficult to like. I'm not giving you this information to hurt you. I mean it constructively; think of it as flash feedback."

She squeezed the remaining mastic gum from the toothpaste tube. She hated concept desserts.

"I didn't ask for your view, and unsolicited feedback is kind of rude, just so you know." She slurred slightly as she spoke.

Freddie heard the slurring more than he heard the words and looked at her with the smugness of someone who had sworn off alcohol and no longer craved it (though, in fact, he was neither).

"Are you alright," he asked her, knowing that was all that was needed, and right on cue, that is when she lost it.

Although Toby and Cordelia were unaware of it at the time, it would bring them some comfort to find out later each of them smashed glassware that evening.

Cordelia limited herself to one water glass, but given the public setting, she felt it was sufficient. Toby would later tell her she should have smashed everything in sight, that it was cathartic and that he would recommend it, but Cordelia was prone to playing the long game, and was already worried about the civil liability implications.

It hadn't been as bad as their worst fights, she reasoned—the ones when they yelled at each other for hours, slamming doors, retreating to different parts of their home before reconvening for more—and she distrusted couples who didn't fight, or who claimed not to. Part of her liked the drama; it reminded her she was alive. Freddie found this difficult. He thought not succumbing to the dramatic was a sign of self-worth: he had grown up in a household where the prevailing emotion was terrible, inconsolable upset and he was determined not to let history repeat itself; his childhood had taught him tears aren't particularly effective other than to confirm someone's lurking suspicion you really are that weak.

Freddie was standing on the parasol area immediately outside their room. He was looking out onto the sea, intent on returning to London that night. He regretted ordering the third bottle of wine, but the service was slow, and, caught up in the moment, it seemed a good idea at the time. In the distance, he saw Cordelia making her approach. She seemed to have recovered her poise, but when he saw her up close, he could see her distress: the skin on her face looked stretched, and her eyes were slightly bloodshot. Part of him pitied her inability to camouflage herself.

"The most mortifying part is their apology," she said, laughing a little. "As if there was something so bad about the service, the only appropriate response was smashing their glassware."

"Amusing," he said.

"They thought you didn't like the food," she continued, "that you stormed off because the food was sub-standard."

She opened the door to their suite, taking three attempts, turned on one of the table lamps, and came back out of the room without her dress.

"You really are terrible, you know."

Of all the things they said to each other that night, Cordelia didn't say the one thing she'd planned on saying. The thought of it, its enormity, its destructive influence, all of it, all of it made her wretched.

*

Mrs. Green was sitting on the plane, facing backwards, and looking forward to the flight. It had been a long trip and she wanted home. She broke the habit of a lifetime and accepted a glass of champagne, which she drank tentatively and with a feeling she was going off the rails. It was a bumpy take-off—expect a nibble of turbulence, the captain warned them as they taxied to the runway—and she clutched at her pearls as the engines forced their way through the cloud and the loose metal in the galleys clattered around. She looked at the other passengers. They were young, everyone seemed younger these days, and sort of entitled looking. Most were on their phones. Two were on their phones right till take-off. The staff had to tell them three times to stop and still they were indignant. There were too many mothers struggling with their children, none of them doing a particularly good job of it. They fought over the bassinet and a steward had to intervene. Mrs. Green turned her attention to the millennial whose carry-on luggage bore gold tags. She knew as soon as he sat down, she was sitting next to Professor Self's son, but he hadn't noticed and when they started speaking, he didn't recognise her from the supper. Boys are so self-centred at that age, she thought, at any age, really. He talked at her a lot, but he wasn't without charm, and she could see his appeal. At one point, he seemed to move himself to tears, and she offered him one of the monographed cotton handkerchiefs bearing Henry's initials, glad to be rid of it. She liked the idea of his precious cloth being used by a lithe and nubile young man. When she spoke to him, she adopted an earnest and worldly outlook she didn't really believe.

Pop music played over the tannoy in the queue for passport control, a female voice singing about feeling sexual. The driver collected her at the gate and returned her home.

One of the girls was in, fussing in the kitchen.

Mrs. Green left her luggage in the hallway for one of them to unpack, whenever that would be, and quietly but fastidiously inspected each of the rooms. She had been away five weeks, a new record; she preferred not to leave it that long, but needs must, and these were extraordinary circumstances.

She loved this house. She loved everything about it. She loved its solidity, and the sense of possibility it once had. She had lived here most of her life. She and Henry, it had grown with them, and it would decline with them too.

To her frustration, everything seemed in order. It all looked as when she'd left, only smaller, somehow. She looked for points she could make to the girls anyway; the dusty underside of the shutters, the ironed shirts on hangers without the top buttons done up.

She was exhausted and retired to bed without enquiring as to Henry's whereabouts. He was probably in surgery, uncontactable. As long as he was back for tomorrow; Freddie had asked to see them, and she didn't want to face him on her own. She had put it in his diary, and they had discussed it briefly. She suspected Cordelia had left him. Stupid girl, she thought, it's exactly the sort of reckless, self-defeating decision she would make. Mrs. Green wished someone had told her parenting never ends, just its requirements change. She thought it was easier when she could insulate her from the world and invite in only the bits she knew she would like. Not that she disliked Freddie.

He had an unknowability which made it difficult to be quite sure what he was thinking. She liked that in a man. There was something held back about him, like he wanted something from you but wasn't going to tell you what.

She slept well and woke to the cat padding up and down her left side, purring, either content or hungry, or both. Downstairs, Henry was already seated at the breakfast table, scooping out the gloopy remains of egg white from its shell. The bald part of his head sometimes reminded her of a boiled egg. He was a fat old man these days, but he hadn't always been, and when she looked at him and was in the right frame of mind, she could still see a glimmer of the man he once was. He used to fuck her right here on the breakfast table. It had collapsed twice, and they'd had to have it reinforced. She remembered telling the carpenter it broke when she was kneading dough, that she didn't know her own strength.

Henry was working on a paper, but they exchanged the briefest of pleasantries and sat side by side in comfortable silence. He was wearing one of the new checked shirts she had left out for him. It suited his complexion; she knew it would as soon as she saw it. She'd bought all eight colours. Once she found a formula which worked, she stuck to it.

When Freddie rang the doorbell, Henry was still deep in thought. As he aged, it became increasingly easy to read his emotional state from the wrinkles on his forehead.

"Be pleasant," she said, touching his arm for emphasis.

Freddie took a deep breath. They were expecting him, but they made him wait because they knew he would.

He stood back from the door and inspected the two bay trees planted either side of it. Their galvanised steel boxes glinted in the sun as he checked the time in the message. He had not misremembered. Four minutes passed, but he decided not to ring the doorbell again. Someone on the inside of the house tried to open the door but it was locked. The door rattled in its frame and the lock moved about in its casing. Freddie looked down at the black and white mosaic tiles. He found their geometry reassuring.

"Where is the bloody key," Mr. Green said quite loudly from inside the hallway, stomping around in frustration. Someone found it, gave it to him and Freddie heard him ram it into the lock. The door opened.

"Ah, Freddie!" He said it like he was surprised. "Do come in."

Mr. Green continued to hold onto the door, but he stepped to one side to make room.

"You'll take off your shoes?"

It wasn't a question.

Freddie stepped onto the entrance mat which had been built into the parquet floor and tried to remove his brogues. There was nowhere to sit. He untied one lace but the other tangled itself into a small, stubborn knot which left him half a centimetre short of the room he needed to slip off the shoe with any sort of grace.

It was a house which conveyed formality, and its owners required it of anyone under its roof. Cordelia had told him as much; family breakfast each morning with eggs, dressing for dinner, talking heads long into the night.

Mr. Green sat next to Mrs. Green and Freddie sat opposite them, positioning himself uncomfortably between two seat cushions. He tucked his feet under the footstool; there was a hole in one of his socks, and the other had a bleach stain. Mr. and Mrs. Green looked at Freddie and Freddie looked at them. He thought they looked like Bert and Ernie, but with less enthusiasm for life. Everything they did was painfully slow, decisions were postponed for years and eventually abandoned.

"May we offer you something?" Mrs. Green asked him.

"Maybe a Xanax, if you have one."

Mr. Green looked at him expressionless. Freddie thought of him as a man for whom a Venn diagram was a mark of creativity.

Mrs. Green averted her eyes.

How he hated them, their lives of carefully calibrated rewards. He'd tried everything to win them over, sent them flowers, sent them claret. Mr. Green never even said thank you; if it was raised at all, his expression was so blank it was clear he had no idea Freddie had even bothered. Freddie found it strange he didn't have the good grace just to play along.

"Perhaps you would like some Darjeeling?" Mr. Green continued. "Or perhaps another type of tea. We are building quite the collection."

"Oh my, yes," said Mrs. Green. "There are so many to pick from, these days."

"A friend of mine has been recommending Sobacha. He discovered it in San Francisco."

"I don't think we have that one," Mrs. Green said to Mr. Green, worried.

"I just meant you're right, there are so many, nowadays."

Freddie felt everything they had ever said to each other was one long misunderstanding.

Nobody moved, and after a moment of excruciating silence, Freddie asked them if they would like him to make it. Mrs. Green gave him a patrician stare. She didn't like men who were too good at explaining.

"One of the girls will do it," she advised him.

Freddie wondered who the girls were, and where the Greens kept them.

41

"Did you and Cordelia have a lovely time in Amalfi?" asked Mrs. Green.

"We did. It's lovely there at this time of year."

"Late September is better," said Mr. Green. They liked to travel off-season so they could shiver on the beach all by themselves.

Freddie hadn't spent much time with Cordelia's parents, and he had never not done so without Cordelia. They could be hard work, but hard work was something Freddie and Mr. and Mrs. Green all believed in, they had that much in common. And Cordelia, of course. They had her in common as well.

"How is Cordelia," Freddie asked, directing his attention to Mrs. Green.

She looked at him. He waited for her to speak. She looked like she was trying to, so he waited.

"I'm terribly sorry," Mrs. Green started to say. It was a turn of phrase; she never apologised, and she never explained, but sometimes it helped her get her sentences up and running. "You're asking me for information about Cordelia?"

Freddie had prepared for this, but couldn't quite remember how to start, and a different beginning made it difficult to trace his way back to the phraseology he'd rehearsed.

"I appreciate she may not want to speak to me, but it's been a week. It's taken a lot to swallow my pride and knock on your door." His voice cracked.

"What in God's name do you mean?" Mr. Green's face looked like an exclamation mark. He spoke with the authority of a man who was totally, genuinely, convinced he deserved all he had.

"Perhaps we're talking at crossed purposes," Freddie's way of saying he had made himself perfectly clear. "If she's asked you not to speak with me, I rather hoped you might just tell me anyway."

He gave them a smile which wasn't returned. He could hear the grandfather clock on the first-floor landing.

"Do you mean to say you have not heard from Cordelia in over a week and you think we have?" Mr. Green asked him, trying unsuccessfully not to raise his voice.

"Mr. Green, that's what I said."

"Freddie, that is not what you said and now we have established what it is you should have said as soon as I opened the door to you, the question is where the hell is she?"

As he spoke, one of the girls appeared with a tray of teacups and a selection of tea bags. Mr. Green told her to get out. The girl seemed not in the least surprised by the command, or the word choice, or the tone.

Freddie took a deep breath. "I rather had the impression she received some news which had upset her."

"She had," Mrs. Green replied.

"May I ask for information about that news?"

"It's a family matter." The Greens didn't like to say no, and usually were quite skilled in making clear that the answer was no without having to use either the word or any of its synonyms. Freddie rather admired them for this, but it hadn't occurred to him that one day they would deploy the strategy on him.

"Won't you sit down, Henry," she asked. "We can track her phone."

"You mean this phone?" Freddie reached into his pocket and placed the device on the footstool.

Mrs. Green stared at it.

"May I ask if she has done something like this before?" Freddie asked her.

"Not that I can recall," she replied, lying.

43

Mr. Green, who had been pacing back and forth along one of the front-facing windows, sat back down on the sofa and leaned forward, interlocking his fingers.

"I'm sorry to say it, but it rather looks like she's left you," he said to Freddie, looking straight at him. He spoke without sympathy.

"Why do you assume it's from me she's running away?"

| PART TWO |
THE MEMORY OF A LOSS

2014—2017

Dear Seb,

It's our anniversary! One year since you told me you'd met someone else and would be leaving that night.

You told me I'd be heartbroken. Thank you for telling me how I would feel. You were right, of course. I was heartbroken. And lost, and humiliated, and flailing around in the dark. I still feel like that sometimes, but I don't feel the loss so much as the memory of the loss, reminding me to stay vigilant, and never to forget.

At first, I thought I could change your mind. I had before. I suggested couples' therapy or giving you space. I said go travelling, I'll pay. You weren't interested. Eventually I persuaded you to stay the night, but you fell asleep quickly, and that's when I knew. I remember looking at you incredulously and wondering who you were. Later, I would try to find out. I searched your name online. I read your tweets. I learned you had been in Edinburgh for the day and that you had eaten your body weight in pasta. It was barely a month after you'd left, and I was eating almost nothing at all. I saw a photo of you watching a play. You were drinking a bottle of Budvar. You were wearing glasses and looked gaunt. You wore clothes I didn't recognise. Everything was different to the person you were with me.

But it was also a version of the you I had known. You were so capable and interested. You navigated the world in ways I never could. You opened my eyes to what was possible, then cast me adrift.

I dug around for evidence of someone else. I wanted proof, and I found it amongst the possessions you left behind, amongst your fancy dress costumes, your dick picks, your university notes. It was a love poem, something about him radiating an energy you once knew. It was quite good, actually. There were multiple drafts. It was a labour of love. You probably wrote it at my desk. You certainly weren't worried about me finding it.

I still wonder why you did it. It was so unnecessary, and I'll never know which bits of us were lies. I can just about see why some married men have affairs. The tedium of daily life, slaving away at some little job which doesn't matter, to make enough money to pay the mortgage for a house they never see. Those men are locked in. You weren't. You could have left at any time you chose. That you did what you did despite that freedom makes me feel used in a particularly manipulative way.

I wondered what it was like for you in the months after you left. You wouldn't have felt what I felt, but you must have felt something. I'd offered you my life. I had nothing bigger to give.

I still know your phone number by heart, but I have never called you and doubt I ever will. I thought you might get in touch, eventually. But my birthday, a couple of weeks after you left, came and went, as did Christmas, as did what would have been our anniversary, they all passed and still you remained silent.

It is like the person I knew has died. Sometimes I dream you have, just so I can remember you as you were then, frozen in time. In my dreams, I pretend you were telling me the truth.

Yours,
Tristan

THE JOURNAL OF SEBASTIAN SELF

8 July 2014

I am on the Buquebus. It's five am and there are too many people. I was planning to sleep all the way to Montevideo, but there's a family sandwiched around me, eating cheese. Day trip, probably. The son isn't bad. Caught him looking a couple of times. Seems to find his mother as overbearing as I do. Does she ever stop talking? If he spoke English, I would ask him.

Not sure what to expect from Uruguay. A little company would be nice.

I wish Tristan were here.

9 July 2014

The hotel is cheap as chips, but there's no laundry service, which is a problem because I am running out of clothes. Had a quick wander round what I thought was the town centre, but hopefully I'm mistaken because it was run down and felt a bit dangerous. No one around. No cafes. Just crumbling buildings and shops selling unlocked phones.

11 July 2014

Woke up hungover and starved. Nothing open so gorged on a buffet breakfast in the Marriot. Expensive, but worth it. The place was full of suits and pilots. The glamour of international travel. Whatever it is I want, it isn't that.

12 July 2014

Am in the Teatro Solis drinking white wine. Had a tour of the place. Well, me and twenty others, divided up by language. No takers for English but for me and a German girl who said the Spanish tour guide spoke too quickly for her to keep up. She wanted to hang out, but I'd rather sit here and drink. Would have been nice to hang out with the tour guide, though. I like theatre boys. And he had a knack for idioms.

14 July 2014

On a bus to Punta del Este wearing a damp polo shirt I rinsed out in a sink and dried with a hairdryer.

Flicked through one of the books Tristan told me to read. Managed ten pages before giving up. What does he see in this stuff?

15 July 2014

It's off-season and no one is here. Walked along the beach for three hours amongst the empty deckchairs and boarded up beach bars. The hotel is dealing with my laundry. Sixty dollars for the expedited service but I can't face staying here for more than one night.

17 July 2014

I arrived in Colonia del Sacramento to discover Tristan's letter awaiting me. I can hear his voice in it and read it over and over and over.

Love this place! Spent the day taking photos. One in fifteen is a winner; I took over a thousand and will edit them tonight.

Some random girls in a café recognised me from the Buquebus. I didn't remember them, but their story checked out. They had very specific knowledge about where I was sitting and the family that smelled of cheese. I assumed they were forever friends but turns out they just met. One was finishing up her trip, the other was just getting started and heading to Brazil. Nice girls, but vacuous. One clearly wanted me to fuck her.

19 July 2014

I am growing tired of no one speaking English. Every transaction is an ordeal. Dining is especially difficult. I never know what I'll be served. Increasingly I just take what I'm given and am grateful. The Tannat helps.

Wandering around, you start to see the same people, doing the same things they were yesterday. I want to ask them why.

Only two nights before the solo part of this trip comes to an end. Wish I'd made more of it, but it's not for me. Useful to know. Turns out they were right.

20 July 2014

Back in Buenos Aires and in the mood for fun.

My body is looking quite good at the moment. I haven't worked out for weeks, but the stress of fending for myself has burned off the fat.

Went to a very late starting underwear party, the place full of good-looking boys. Got with a couple of them, but the best bit was watching some guy getting tossed off, pants round his ankles and staring straight at me. When he came, his whole body vibrated.

21 July 2014

Camilla is here, and her insane amount of luggage. We're planning to hang out here for a couple of days, take in the sights. To be honest, I would kill for an early night. So tired suddenly.

3 August 2014

I've been too busy to write. Camilla's fault. It's been gnawing away at me, knowing I was falling behind. Things I saw, or thought about, which it would have been useful to write down, gone now, consumed and discarded. So much of our lives are lost to oblivion because no one ever took the trouble to write it down. Must make more of an effort to keep up.

It's been lovely, though. Truly. We've extended our stay here twice. We're still in Buenos Aires and have no plans to leave. Haven't felt this great in ages. I'm trying to think of all the stuff we've done, the detail of it, but all I can summon is a warm fuzzy feeling and I look up and everything I see is in sharp focus and I think, yes, this is what life is meant to be.

6 August 2014

We have had the most enormous fight and I am on a bus out of here, alone.

7 August 2014

Still on the bus. But there is wine, there is food and there is a seat which folds flat, so I can sleep. Fifteen messages from Camilla. Full marks for perseverance. I have replied, against my better judgement; she is following me to Iguazu Falls.

10 August 2014

Iguazu Falls, full of people I'd rather not know existed.

"You have a cute butterfly on you, it's landed on your sunglasses. Let's all take a photo." No thanks.

"Will you take a photo of me and my mum so we can celebrate our ugliness?" No. Get away from me.

Stayed up drinking at the bar, where I write this. The waiter keeps giving me double measures. I wonder what else he will do to cheer me up.

14 August 2014

Today we bicycled around some Mendoza vineyards and drank our body weight in wine. Camilla was roaringly drunk and on the best form. It's a life skill, though wonders at what cost.

We joined up with four backpackers who are staying at our hostel. They are sitting in front of me now. The boy is hot, but I see now he's into girls and is trying to get with Camilla. She is having none of it. He doesn't stand a chance. For one thing, he's not fifty. And he's not independently wealthy, for another.

19 August 2014

We are sharing a room in Valparaiso, having checked in as husband and wife. It was spur of the moment: it's a couples' place, and the owner is nicer to us now she thinks we're young and in love.

The prospect of sharing a bed with Camilla is freaking me out. We're close, but not that close. Camilla seems fine about it. Unperturbed, as father would put it. But I like my space, and I don't know if I have any strange sleeping habits she will use against me when I least expect it.

We spent the afternoon wandering around the cobbled streets, doing impressions of people we know. The quadrants here are so pretty and artisan. Tristan would like them. I bought him a bracelet.

The sun is setting, and we are drinking strong gin and tonics from the honesty bar. We are sitting on the veranda and Camilla has just told me I should abandon the premise of everything I have ever known. I told her she should switch to vodka.

20 August 2014

Camilla turned in early, was fast asleep once I made it to the room, and snored like a tiger pistol shrimp the whole night. I have taken a recording.

21 August 2014

Today we took tentative steps towards exploring off the beaten track, including a hair-raising trip in a rusting funicular. We made it to the coast, realised it was rough as, quickly scarpered up the hill, then got lost in a bit of town full of graffiti.

I thought there might be scope to feast with the panthers, but the ever-resourceful Camilla found a man willing to drive us to civilisation, so here we are, back where we were yesterday, safe and sound and about to select a bottle of something chilled and expensive to drink in the sun.

I point out to Camilla we do exactly what we would be doing in San Francisco. Unfair, she says, we're broadening our horizons, and the effect is cumulative. But I wonder. Sometimes it feels like we could be anywhere. But we are here, and it is pretty, and the wine is perfectly chilled.

23 August 2014

Camilla has persuaded me to take a detour so we can stay in a hotel which looks like a boat. So here we are, in Vina del Mar. The couple at the table next to us are Scottish, though I can't tell from which bit and thought it might be rude to ask. They don't sound like Tristan.

24 August 2014

Santiago, our final stop. I suggested to Camilla we reward ourselves for slumming it in hostels by going five stars for the final stretch. She didn't need much persuasion, although she did point out we have only stayed in two hostels and only for two nights at that. Two nights too many, if you ask me. The hotel is fine, but it is the sort of place father would insist on when attending one of his many conferences. Or guest lecturing, or whatever it is he does to spend time away from home. Supper was ruined by a table of entitled yobs barking orders at the waitress. The mother was particularly obnoxious, her dirty money and perfect teeth.

27 August 2014

I abandoned Camilla in a club and went off with some guy. My bad. But he was beautiful, and local, and at least now I can say I've been rimmed by a Chilean national.

1 September 2014

We are back in San Francisco, and everyone is packing up. Mother and father are returning to the East Coast, and I leave for Edinburgh at the end of the week. Father has changed his tune while we were absent. Now he goes out of his way to support my decision, says every young man must forge his own path. We shall see if it lasts. He hasn't once asked if we had fun in South America, though he has paid off the debt on my cards, which is something. He objected to us having flown business, but other than that, no complaints. I've barely seen Camilla since we returned, despite both of us living under the same roof. She seems a different person here. Or maybe I just need her less.

3 September 2014

I do hate packing. It seems so pointless. There will be shops, one assumes. Mother has organised a farewell supper, the guest list for which includes four people I've never met. When I pointed this out, she said I had a lot to learn. I made a special request for set custard and rhubarb jelly. She said I have the tastes of a child but would mention it to the caterers.

5 September 2014

I spoke with a lovely woman on the plane. I still have her husband's handkerchief.

She said if she knew one thing about being sixty-five, it was there's no use pretending to be someone you're not, that it never works. She said she didn't know why people made such a fuss about these things.

6 September 2014

I didn't realise my connection left from City, so I missed it and I missed the flight after that as well. Tristan is annoyed. He was already at the airport, but I'd been travelling for fifteen hours and the thought of getting on another plane tonight was more than I could handle. He hung up on me when I told him, which was nice of him and not at all selfish.

8 September 2014

Being with Tristan again, touching him again, it is—everything. We know so much about each other already.

I do feel on the backfoot, though. This is his habitat.

I'm moving into halls once term starts. I'll stay at his place till then, if there is space for me amongst all the books, that is. I mean, they are everywhere—on the floors, in the kitchen dresser where the glassware should be, in the bathroom next to the shower. He has a TV at least, though no WIFI.

10 September 2014

Tristan is at work, litigating for the corporations, so I have spent the last two days wandering the streets. I feel like I know them already, that I have seen them before. There aren't all that many. I'm frightened by the prospect it's as small as I think it might be. What have I done?

15 September 2014

Term has started, finally. Three lectures back-to-back, all well-attended. Father is on the reading list.

18 September 2014

I attended my first seminar. A room of twenty students and a tutor who graduated two years ago. Unacceptable.

15 October 2014

I love Tristan as I have never loved anyone; his oddness, his beautiful freakery, the way he smiles.

4 November 2014

I spend my mornings in George Square, being lectured to by people of varying abilities. My favourite is a tall blonde woman, who looks and sounds Swedish. She talks a lot about Kant but pronounces it Cunt. "Without Cunt, the path of twentieth century Western philosophy would have paid little attention to feminist political discourse." "Cunt recognises the synonymy of individual happiness and the promotion of ethical behaviour." "We should ask ourselves what role Cunt can play in the betterment of communal living." She is oblivious and I hope no one tells her.

My afternoons are spent in the main library, the one that looks like a disused car park. It helps that most of the students in the library are not there to work. They circle the room, looking for people they know, to make plans, and to flirt. The assignments take time, but they don't take forever. It comes easily.

I never made it into Halls. I was booked in, allocated a room, but took one look at it and said no. It was small and clinical and looked like a prison cell. Camilla says I should have stuck it out, that it's not about the rooms, it's about the people and the more people I meet, the better. Quantity, not quality?

I thought about just staying with Tristan. He would love it. I would love it. But it's too soon. I need my own space. I'm looking for somewhere, but term has already started so it won't be easy.

12 November 2014

It's been an interesting tour of the student ghetto. There are worse places to be than the sandstone tenements of Marchmont. I've found a place I like. Some guy got himself kicked off his course, so I get his room. I move in Tuesday.

13 November 2014

Turns out one of Tristan's friends is my new neighbour. Toby. Owns the place next door.

1 December 2014

Tristan is turning me into a film buff. We meet in the Film House on Lothian Road, where we gorge on vegetable lasagne, drink red wine, and watch something with subtitles. He arrives straight from his office, tired, his hair looking funked.

2 January 2015

My flat mates are throwing a house party in my honour, which is nice of them. They asked if I wanted to invite Tristan. I said no. I have, however, invited Toby. I did it on a whim. He just happened to be at his front door as I was passing. I took the lead. I had to. He's shy. We talked for about ten minutes, circling around each other, each unsure what the other knew. He gave very little away. I admire that.

7 January 2015

Edinburgh is starting to feel like home. Turns out all I needed was a house party and some creature comforts. I've bought some cashmere blankets to drape around myself as the evenings close in and the air turns chilly.

Toby came after all. I didn't think he would, but I suppose he doesn't know all that many people now he's relocated, so he says yes to everything and hopes something will stick. That's what I would do. Am doing.

He arrived late, clutching two bottles of wine, one under each arm. I took them from him, inspected the labels and said they looked too expensive for a house party. I thought he would play along and tell me he only buys expensive wine and that I should too. That's what Tristan would say. So would my father, for that matter. But my comment embarrassed him, and he blushed.

He asked if Tristan was coming. I wasn't sure how to play it, but I knew not to lie. So, I told him, sometimes it's good to talk to new people, and then I took him by the arm and introduced him to two of my flatmates. I told them Toby lives downstairs and he was here to complain about the noise.

12 January 2015

I return after the weekend looking pale and exhausted and still slightly drugged. Invariably Tristan is turned on by this and tries to initiate.

14 January 2015

Some guy just tried to pick me up in a coffee shop opposite Old College. We were standing in line; he said he wanted to pay for me 'by using his card'. I asked him for a flat white and told him to carry cash next time.

15 January 2015

The students in my classes take everything so seriously, and the questions they ask are so pedantic. They quote footnotes and type non-stop, getting the point down verbatim, getting their money's worth.

I ask Toby if this is what it was like for him. He says probably.

This, I am learning, is typical of him. He never misses an opportunity to avoid committing himself to a point. When did he become afraid of his own shadow?

16 January 2015

Toby invited me in for a glass of wine. He has a nice place, although you can hear the students upstairs, living a different life. It's a matter of when, not if, the bass starts thumping.

I like listening to Toby. There is something so interesting about people who are fucked up psychologically.

19 January 2015

Mr. Minimum Spend was in the library. He didn't look like he was there to work. He looked like he was looking for somebody—not for me, he insisted—but I told him my name and he's messaged me: "It would be fun to hang out."

22 January 2015

Tristan suggested we go on a double date with Toby and some guy he is seeing. What?

26 January 2015

It was interesting to see Tristan and Toby interact. They're close, you can see that, and they're comfortable in each other's company, and they don't try to impress each other, which I like. But they're also careful with their words, and bite their tongue when something has angered them. It's not a friendship I would want.

It was fun meeting Dominick. Very pretty. Brown hair, pale alabaster skin. We got smashed at the bar when Tristan and Toby started talking shop.

10 February 2015

I'm exhausted. I'm out every night, either at Tristan's, or wherever.

The cinema trips are long gone, incidentally. His working hours don't allow it. So instead, we stay home and cook with the ingredients I have bought, and we watch box sets on TV until he falls asleep on the sofa.

What I really need is a couple of days to myself, but instead, I arrange to meet Mr. Minimum Spend and end up in his bed.

12 February 2015

I had a go at Toby for not telling me about Dominick. He said I wasn't in a position to negotiate terms.

We were still bickering as we walked through the meadows. It was dark, but sports teams were practising on the grass, shouting at each other, and competing, taking all the fun out of it. We must have looked an odd pair. Toby with his suit and satchel, me without those things.

He made me an industrial strength Tanqueray and tonic, which tasted like paint stripper, and we drank them in his freshly decorated lounge, on the saddle nut brown Chesterfield delivered from his London place yesterday.

When I sit in a room like this, I feel protected from the world and never want to leave.

As I left, he put his hands on my hips and said Tristan must never know. "He doesn't see these things the way you and I do."

14 February 2015

The Minimum Spend is pushing for anal. I suspect he would be quite good at it, and he was shy when he raised it, which was appealing. I'll have to tell Tristan I want to start using condoms.

15 April 2015

All the ledger entries in my accounts are debits, which can't be good. Rent is due tomorrow and that will wipe me out entirely. I tried to cancel the standing order, but it was too late.

Father and I don't discuss money, specifically, but it would have been perfectly clear to him I require funds. I'm not self-made, after all, and it's much cheaper for me to be here than at his precious Harvard. It's probably a banking error.

17 April 2015

Not a banking error. It's a message. Well, fuck him.

19 April 2015

I mentioned my money problem to Tristan. We've never discussed money before. I didn't specifically ask for some of his, and he didn't offer any of it, anyway. But I told him, if I must get a job, we won't spend as much time together.

21 April 2015

The Minimum Spend is around during the day, which is nice. Most of our time we spend in his flat in Marchmont, watching Family Guy and having sex.

11 May 2015

I invited Tristan to a gig in the Cowgate last week. One of my flatmates was doing a set, so we were all there to show our support and to drink cheap beer. They knew Tristan was coming and they teased me. *Boyfriend!*

The introductions were painful. Tristan insisted on shaking their hands and repeating their names back to them. I couldn't look anyone in the eye and downed three double vodkas before anyone had played a note.

Only when the music started did I realised Tristan was nervous. He sat on a bench near the bass guitarist, tapping the table, the beat eluding him. It would have helped if the music was better. I felt responsible, and feared Tristan would shout at me later for wasting his time. He does that sometimes, but not this time: all he said was he was glad I wanted him there and that he'd like to do it again. The others could have made more of an effort with him if I'm honest.

21 May 2015

I pointed out to the Minimum Spend that we never go out. We just hang out at his place. We were in the kitchen at the time, and he responded by pulling my pants down and bending me over the kitchen counter, which shut me up pretty fast.

28 May 2015

Tristan has gonorrhoea but believed my spin on the science. He bought me a fragrance I don't like by way of apology.

23 June 2015

I have been offered employment. The job description is vague, but I was flattered into doing it, and research assistant sounds better than bartender. Otto, or Professor Stewart as he is known to those who lack the confidence to call him by his name, told me he was impressed by the quality of my work. He is in the market for a footnote checker, but it can't be just anyone, apparently; he needs someone who really understands how he sees the world and the place of the philosopher in it, and that was when—apparently—he thought of me. I tried to play hard to get, but he had me at hello, and he knew it.

25 June 2015

A night in my bedroom, alone. It feels like it belongs to someone else, so little time do I spend in it. It's 20:00 and the prospect of three hours in my own company terrifies me. This can't be normal.

26 June 2015

I made it to 21:30 before knocking on Toby's front door. It didn't occur to me Dominick might be there. He wasn't, but Toby told me I should think about these things. He invited me in, on the condition I sit on the sofa quietly and not disturb him.

He was half through *Husbands and Wives*, his favourite Woody Allen, and determined to finish it.

I saw it through to the end, and as soon as the credits started to roll, I told him he looked tired. He blamed the one-hundred-hour billable week. The thing is, I would be very surprised if he actually works that and, if he does, why did he bother leaving London? This annoyed him. It's the first time he's shown me his anger. "Edinburgh isn't the provinces!" he informed me, shouting. I told him I knew that.

29 July 2015

Otto is writing about the nature of truth. My task is to check his footnotes. It is time-consuming, difficult work. There are thousands of them, and they are, without exception, a mess. The first thing I do is take a deep breath and then I sit down and work my way through them methodically, fighting down the urge to feel overwhelmed. Most of them require a detailed working knowledge of intersubjectivity, which I don't have and am not particularly interested in acquiring. I wish Otto had told me before I signed up. Why don't people just tell me what they want from me? Do they think they're too clever not to talk in code?

6 August 2015

The Minimum Spend is out of town for reasons unknown, so I have spent the week alternating between Tristan and Toby. It suits me, and them. They are both dog-tired by the time I am summoned, another ten-hour day behind them spent servicing something they say is important, so once every two nights is more than plenty. They are tired, but also there is euphoria, the satisfaction of hard work, of keeping the show on the road.

When it is like this, they are almost identical. They tell me about their day, another version of the events I heard the night before. I listen and what I want to say is: no, that is not what it was like at all.

15 August 2015

I am giving up reading anything by anyone alive. You know where you stand with the dead. They have said what they have to say, and they won't let you down by changing their mind. Camilla gives it a week.

7 September 2015

My flatmates have asked me to move out. They say they want someone who is more committed to flat life and by that they mean someone who actually spends time there.

8 September 2015

When it started to unfold, what struck me most was the banality of it all. Just because it's low-key, doesn't mean it isn't a big deal, I guess.

Here's the thing; we wouldn't have been there at all but for Tristan. He's got a bee in his bonnet about seeking out the new, the latest instalment of which meant eating soft shell tacos in a restaurant where the Minimum Spend waits on tables. He hadn't even told me he had a job! Why not even mention it? I know what it takes to keep something hidden from view, and I can usually tell when someone is keeping something from me. I know what to look for.

So suddenly, there he was with his little notepad asking if it was a special occasion, to which Tristan of course replied that we'd been together so long we were way past date nights. The Minimum Spend, to his credit, didn't flinch. I thought the best thing to do was to acknowledge that we knew each other. But he didn't want to play along.

"No, it seems I don't know you at all," was all he said, but his tone was flippant, and Tristan thought he was flirting. We had three courses, but I can't remember any of them.

9 September 2015

He says he will tell Tristan. I told him not to be ridiculous, but I can't be sure he won't, and I am beginning to panic.

10 September 2015

Coming clean was the only option.

I told Tristan our relationship is over, that I did something months ago which I shouldn't have, and now it was being used against me. I had prepared what I wanted to say, but my voice shook as I delivered my lines.

He wanted details, but I said there was no point. "I'm not as good a person as you think I am," I told him. "Not everyone likes me."

He has flu, but he was calm, took a deep breath and said he didn't see why the relationship had to end.

"Just tell people we have an open relationship," he said, before emphasising we don't.

I'm sitting on my bed, feeling frozen.

Is this what it's like to be free?

21 September 2015

A week has passed, and my indiscretions have been swept under the rug. It is business as usual. The ease with which Tristan has forgiven me is unsettling. Camilla says it is low self-esteem.

But it does feel like a fresh start. There is something here which is worthwhile. I still feel so much for him, and I regret hurting him, and he is hurt, I can see that.

1 October 2015

The atmosphere in the apartment is toxic. I intended to fix it, but if they won't meet me halfway, I'm more than happy to make it difficult for them. Camilla joked I should sub-let my room to someone hideous.

3 October 2015

I am making a conscious effort to carve out more time to spend with Tristan and am avoiding Toby. It's possible he knows nothing. Tristan is proud and stubborn, and he won't make himself vulnerable unless all is lost and he is out of options.

We don't talk about it. So much of what we have together exists in unspoken space.

5 October 2015

When I signed up to work with Otto, I didn't know he had a reputation for being difficult. I've lost count of the people taking me aside to "inform" me. I nod along and make reassuring noises but, really, it amazes, all these people, their axes to grind. What they don't like is success, or what it takes to excel.

In any event, Otto has his favourites, and I am one of them, at least for the time being, so I just need to hope no one younger or prettier comes along to usurp me. The work I do for him is far from stellar, but he's too polite to say.

"I'll just apply a little polish," is his sort of comment of late, before rewriting it completely.

6 October 2015

Tonight, I suggested we watch *Damages*. Wrong move.

"Why would I want to watch a programme about angry litigators? I spend my whole day doing that," etcetera, etcetera and round and round we went.

"Do what you want," he told me. "You always do."

14 October 2015

I returned home to find a stranger viewing my room. Don't worry, guys, I get the hint. I told him the room was nice, but he'd have to be willing to live with 'these back-stabbing cunts— but, hey, you can't have everything'. They're cowards, too; they couldn't look me in the eye. They just stood there, hands in pockets, asking why I was 'being difficult'. I wanted to give it to them with both barrels, which they deserve, frankly, but I could hear my voice giving way. I excused myself just in time. I rarely cry, but when I do, I really go for it.

Toby found me on the street. He took me in and talked me down, and once he had done that, he took off all my clothes and made me come.

These guys are all the same. They all want someone to save.

11 November 2015

Things have been great with Tristan lately, so I've sort of moved in. Unofficially, no rent or anything, but my clothes are in the wardrobes and my worldly possessions are stacked in the boxroom.

12 January 2016

Camilla has written a play. She wants to bring it to Edinburgh this August, and she wants me to produce it for her. I said I need to read it first.

23 January 2016

Camilla sent me her thing. I don't feature in it *at all*, which is disappointing, and there's no plot, but the dialogue is good. I told Tristan this could be a thing and that I want to be part of it. He didn't say much, but I wouldn't call him supportive.

14 February 2016

Tristan was insistent we exchange Valentine's Day cards, so I bought one, signed my name, and wrote 'Thanks for everything' in it.

17 February 2016

Now we live together, I worry about my privacy. I've spent the morning re-setting my passwords and locking down my profiles. It's instinct, but I keep my phone on me at all times. It comes with me to the bathroom, and I hide it in one of my shoes when we go to bed.

To relax, Tristan likes to sit alone with his thoughts. He places a value on having the time to do that. It is his way of coping with the world, I think, retreating from as much of it as possible. We spend time apart and he is fine with that, I always come back to him and he never asks where I've been, or what I've done. He thinks we're the same, that I need what he needs. He's wrong.

18 February 2016

Camilla will be renting a flat in Marchmont and, logistically, it makes sense I move in with her. I need to tell Tristan, obviously, but I'm picking my moment. Moving in with her doesn't have to mean not living with him.

19 February 2016

Tristan says he always does bits and pieces in the festivals, which is news to me. He never talks about it. This year, he thinks we should go all out with a three-week extravaganza and get some people up from London. It's not a bad idea, but I'll have limited time.

"Baby, it's not as if you wrote the thing," he tells me.

Fair enough. But he's the one building a social life on my coattails.

20 February 2016

I am writing this instead of doing Otto's footnotes. He'll pay me anyway and I'll get around to them eventually. He's good like that. I've started working in his office. At first, I thought he was lonely, but increasingly I think he just likes the sound of his own voice. Some of what he says is interesting and I nod along even if it isn't.

23 February 2016

Tristan asked me how my day was. I said something vague. I would have told him more, but my brain froze and suddenly I couldn't remember. Does he even know I have a job? I flicked through past entries to check but couldn't find the answer. Reading them was unnerving; it doesn't even sound like me, it's more like an echo of a thought. So much is missing. For example, the tenderness of all the quiet moments Tristan and I share, which are golden to me.

I mentioned this to Otto at a faculty event I organised. He seemed surprised I thought a journal could be anything else. I told him, whoever it is I have created, he sounds like a narcissist. Or maybe I just don't like what I see.

24 February 2016

Tristan is trying to be more outgoing, which means I attend dinner parties with people I don't want to meet and whom he barely knows. One of the couples came without her plus one. He's cheating on her, apparently, but she doesn't know, almost wilfully oblivious. Tristan can't stop talking about it.

"How can someone be so blind?" he says.

Meanwhile, work goes from strength to strength, my marks excellent across the board.

25 February 2016

Toby said he had to see me, so I said fine, but insisted we meet in public, i.e., anywhere which is not his flat, nice though it is.

He picked a basement bar in Stockbridge, with candlelight and an array of gins. We sampled four.

I was expecting an exit interview and I think that's what he intended, but one thing led to another, and we ended up in the toilets.

26 February 2016

I'm trying to figure out if it's Toby, or the thrill of sneaking around. Either way, it's transformative. Everything glistens, ripe with possibility. I'm on better form for Tristan, too, so he benefits as well. I feel less beholden to him.

27 February 2016

I live here, but at the same time, not really. This is Tristan's place, his furniture, his tastes, his way of life. I am expected to fit it. I have been telling Otto about my predicament. He rolls his eyes as if to say, 'Was anyone ever so young?'. But he lets me talk. I think he finds it amusing.

1 March 2016

I don't attend as many lectures as I should; I pick and choose from the list, hedging my bets on what sounds interesting, or who on the faculty staff is least likely to notice my absence. I make a point of avoiding Otto's. I'm sitting in the back row looking down, as I write this. None of these people know who I am. They flock about in their groups, making plans. I could have had that.

8 March 2016

The footnotes have been fun, but the project is almost done and I'm not sure how long either of us can continue to string it out. Otto reminds me of Tristan in some ways: confessional, intense, ill at ease.

4 April 2016

I always wanted to be the student who gets fucked by his professor, but it's proving surprising difficult to achieve. Sign of the times, I suppose: puritanical and accusatory. What about *my* needs?

8 April 2016

Now that Toby and I no longer live next door to each other, we message. Or, rather, he tells me he wants me, that he has to have me, and sometimes I reply. It drives him crazy. He says he doesn't like to be left hanging, that he wouldn't put up with it from anyone else.

14 April 2016

Camilla is here, and auditions start tomorrow. It is so wonderful to see her.

20 April 2016

I don't have any experience on the casting couch, but it is definitely fun, the nervous energy in the room notwithstanding.

It's quite the ego trip, and Camilla has told me off at least twice. Authority suits her. Her posture changes and she slows down her breathing.

Most of the candidates were students, a succession of indie boys in identical jeans all trying to convey their uniqueness. There are enough parts for all the ones who can act, though whether they accept the indignity of a smaller role remains to be seen. The ego of boys, and their vanity. Camilla was hoping for some young professionals, but a morning mid-week casting session was always going to make that unlikely. We did get one. A girl called Cordelia. No acting experience, but she was up front about it. Camilla likes her.

28 April 2016

Tristan is oddly distant about the play. I said he could read it, that Camilla wouldn't mind. She likes him a lot. She thinks he's good for me.

17 May 2016

Rehearsals are starting soon, so I'm trying to wrap things up with Otto. He seems reluctant to let me go, but there's only so long I can endure being someone else's sounding board. A life lived in the footnotes. No thank you.

20 May 2016

It's only when I spend time with Camilla that I realise how much I've been missing her. She's probably one of the few people in my life who gets me. She's so capable. She's only been here five minutes and already she's showing *me* around. She's sorted me out money-wise, too. Strictly speaking, it's father's money, but he gave it to her, and she can do with it what she will. Besides, poverty doesn't suit me.

24 May 2016

I've finished up with Otto. The farewell was less than ideal, but I console myself with the knowledge these things are rarely pleasant. He wanted me to stay for longer, to help him with the proofreading, to see the thing through to completion. But it's his project, not mine, and the credit will go to him.

26 May 2016

Today is the first day of rehearsals, all of which will take place in a dispiriting room somewhere in the depths of the Pleasance Courtyard. Camilla is nervous. I am too.

27 May 2016

I suggested post-rehearsal drinks. Good turnout. An arrogant bunch, but chatty, and some of what they say is interesting. People jockeying for position is so exhausting.

Camilla and I walked home together. She told me I needed to make more of an effort with Cordelia. It's important she's made to feel welcome, apparently. I don't see why. Everybody's replaceable when it comes down to it.

28 May 2016

I have so much to do.

I have a list for everything: a list of the people I was supposed to contact yesterday but did not; a list of the books I need to read; a production list which comprises three sub-lists (tasks which are urgent, tasks which are not urgent and tasks which will never be done); a list of the complaints which the cast and crew want to make to Camilla but are too afraid to say to her face. Suddenly, *I'm* the approachable one. I'm as scared of her as they are.

Tristan's nosy, but I close the laptop when he starts to hover.

3 June 2016

The rehearsals are dragging on. The room is too small, too hot, and Camilla is oblivious when she loses the room. If it carries on like this, someone will kick off. That person might be me.

20 June 2016

We've lost three of the cast, two of whom are real losses. They told Camilla where she could stick it. One of them trembled as he shouted at her. Told her she was overbearing (she is) and that she needs to learn how to talk to people (she does), and then he said he would have been willing to overlook who she is if the writing had been better. That's where he lost me. The writing is perfection.

Cordelia suggested I go after them. I mean, what the fuck? I hired *her*. But I stood in the Courtyard, its cobbles greasy with rain, waiting. I got Mark back on board, eventually. He didn't look as full of himself with his legs in the air, writhing around with two of my fingers up his ass. Just before he came, I told him I would provide backstage privileges if he swallowed his pride. He says he's thinking about it but it's a done deal. I've never seen so much cum.

Cordelia is at home, comforting Camilla. There's something off kilter about her. She's too helpful, too eager to please.

21 June 2016

Now that Cordelia has moved in, I have nowhere I can call my own. I'm starting to think Virginia Woolf had a point, though I'd rather slum it in a flat share than live in Bloomsbury. Think how many more turgid novels she could have churned out if she'd had the energy to relocate to somewhere with better architecture.

22 June 2016

Is it better to have sex with someone you don't know or with someone you know too well? The point came up at lunch. I've never seen the appeal of random hook-ups. It always has to mean more.

24 June 2015

Cordelia asked me why I hate her so much. At least she's perceptive.

"Tell me," she said, her voice floating an octave higher than usual. "Hate is always specific."

25 June 2016

Some of my dreams are terrifying. Last night, I was a molecule, coursing through the veins of the universe. The night before that, someone tore off my skin as I danced to a disco beat. Tristan said I woke him up. He found me at the edge of the bed, whimpering in distress as my legs kicked at the air.

26 June 2016

Tristan is inviting some friends to Edinburgh for the festivals. He speaks of Igor with reverential awe, says he is a person around whom things happen, as though he can align the stars and transport us all to a higher realm. It's not magic, I want to tell him. It's a formula.

Camilla says I'm underweight, that my clothes hang off me. I asked her if she could loan me some of her puppy fat.

28 June 2016

Rehearsals are intense, but it's taking shape. The set design is finished. Cordelia made a good job of it. I just wish she'd stop touching my arm every time she talks to me. It makes me nervous.

Toby has cancelled on me twice now, pleading pressure of work.

9 July 2016

Tristan has started booking shows. Five a day, for fifteen days.

9 August 2016

The festivals are in full swing and the city is under siege. Every conceivable outdoor space has been whored into a for-profit venue and I can walk along the streets of the city without fear of bumping into someone I know.

Igor has arrived with his entourage. I'm invited along, because Tristan wants to show me off, but it's all in-jokes. Sometimes, Igor looks at me as if to say, 'Why are you even here?'. He and Tristan put on this show of being the best of friends, but they have nothing in common.

10 August 2016

Ticket sales are low, and Camilla is worried.

She's having flyers printed on Gecko standard paper and wants the cast to hand them out on the Royal Mile. No thank you.

Today I saw five shows with Tristan. A mixed bag. Toby came along to some of them. I asked him if he was still working too hard and he looked at me with this vacant expression which told me he doesn't remember which lie he's told to whom.

16 August 2016

Five stars from *The Scotsman*! Now there is independent corroboration of the play's value, mother and father are flying out to see it.

18 August 2016

Got with Igor in the Underbelly toilets on Cowgate. I like to think it's because I am irresistible, but the reality is he was high, and I was around. He didn't so much touch me as grab at me. For someone who has so much sex, he has surprisingly poor technique.

I spotted Camilla and Cordelia holding hands earlier. Some girls do that sort of thing, I suppose. But it does seem quite gay.

21 August 2016

The cast and crew party was—wild. As the sun came up, Mark made everyone eggs; I am infatuated by him. I'm glad I enticed him back into the fold.

25 August 2016

Tristan is back at work so I'm spending time with Igor. Our days follow the same formula: lazy mornings eating cinnamon buns and teaching ourselves how to work the industrial scale coffee machine in the penthouse he's renting, followed by lunch which lasts most of the afternoon and which is attended by a cast of thousands, most of whom don't seem to have to be anywhere anytime soon, followed by mooching around a gallery or whatever Igor thinks would be good for my education, followed by a nap, then cocktail hour, then out. He does all of this on five hours of sleep. I don't know how. He's starting to wear me out.

29 August 2016

Igor is starting to tire of me, and I of him. We've caned our way through the most phenomenal amount of money doing nothing very much. To be honest, he's not as good-looking as I thought he was. He's thirty-two, and it's starting to show. Crow's feet around the eyes, breath which smells of stale smoke, some other stuff I noticed earlier but can't now remember. To think I was nervous around him when I arrived. I could have made him beg.

31 August 2016

The play has finished, the city is shrinking back to a less inflated version of itself, and I feel wretched. Everyone is saying we'll keep in touch, but, really, what's the point? It will fizzle out into nothing soon enough, as everything does. The one constant in my life is cookie butter, which I eat by the spoonful, straight from the jar.

Before she left, Camilla took me to one side to tell me a few home truths.

"Something is going on here that isn't right."

I asked her to be specific.

She said she couldn't, not yet, but that she knew. I called her Miss Marple and wished her happy sleuthing.

"People aren't playthings, Seb. This stuff matters."

3 September 2016

I've moved back in with Tristan, against my better judgment. He hugged me tightly as I stepped over the threshold, said it's good to have me back, his only acknowledgement I had left.

And so, I suppose life carries on. I'll continue studying, and he'll continue working, and he'll talk about his day as I pour him a glass of wine and then another and another, and as he falls asleep on the sofa, resting against the nook of my arm, I'll ask myself if this is all my life is meant to be.

15 September 2016

Maybe the problem is I'm bored of Edinburgh.

Mark and I see each other most days. I've seen most of his outfits and all his moods. I like the gentleness with which he welcomes in the world, the absence of cynicism about it.

He says, before I write off Scotland, I should at least see more than three streets of it, so he has promised to take me on tour.

"Welcome to Scotland!" he said at the bus stop, with his big grin and that dimple. I can think of worse welcomes.

16 October 2016

Uneventful couple of weeks, working hard but not enjoying it, churning out what is required of me and being told it's good, but the truth is it's lacklustre, plain vanilla stuff and the people telling me otherwise aren't good enough to know the difference. I want to produce work which makes me proud, and which makes my father proud. There. It feels good finally to admit it.

19 October 2016

Tristan has suggested a holiday. My financial situation is less dire than it was but is by no means buoyant. If he pays, I'll go. Sometimes I am amazed how little it takes to keep him satisfied.

20 October 2016

Tristan, he has mellowed. He used to be a lot more difficult. Does it mean he cares less?

But we did fight yesterday, in the cinema, and I stormed out; an act of petulance, I suppose.

What happened to us? He used to electrify me with a single look.

I called Mark, who said I sounded on edge. I played it down, sighing to regain my composure, but his perceptiveness took me aback. He suggested we continue our tour. He took me to Gourock, and to Dunoon, we railed and sailed, and I kissed him on the CalMac ferry, and we talked about how it feels when something comes to an end.

The evidence is in Tristan's flat, if only he cared to look. Part of me thinks I've left it there for him to find. I don't want to hurt him, but there is something contemptuous about the unconditionality of his love.

22 October 2016

We're just people, muddling along as best we can. I will not be made to feel guilty about it.

Tristan and I, we're living together, but not. We're sleeping together, but not. We're in a relationship, but not. People grow apart.

The real problem is this: if Mark finds out, he'll run a mile. He's too good a person to approve of what I've done.

God. I'm beginning to understand why people just get up one morning and vanish.

24 October 2016

I console myself with the possibility Tristan knows, that on some level he wants to set me free.

But he's started leaving property schedules on the coffee table. Houses in the sticks for the straights.

Mark has tickets for *Bon Iver* this Friday, which is more his musical taste than mine, but whatever. I've told Tristan I won't be around. Where does he think I spend all my time?

25 October 2016

Instead of small-talk, I confessed to father every grisly detail. He said I was immature, but also, he was philosophical about my predicament.

"Are you sure?" he asked me.

I didn't answer. Am I?

26 October 2016

Lunch with Mark in the local noodle bar. He told me I am very good at not talking about myself.

"That's because I'm eating," I told him.

"I mean, I don't even know where you live."

I told him he wouldn't like it, which is true.

"There's something about this whole situation which makes me feel I'm your mistress, not your boyfriend."

He's so beautiful, and decent. I love his spindly legs, and his curly blonde hair and his perfect penis.

27 October 2016

Tristan says it is time to start aligning his personal life with his family life. He wants them to know about me and me about them. He's waited thirty years but now it's urgent? His ineptitude angers me, living in his own little land of make-believe.

29 October 2016

Where will I live? Camilla knows a place, but it's nearby.

1 November 2016

A chance encounter with Toby. I gave up on him a long time ago, of course. It's a pity, though. I liked spending time with him.

I said he looked well, which was a lie. He has a sort of heaviness about him.

He wasn't unpleasant. He just made no effort at all, like he has no time for me, like he sees right through me and has decided I'm not worth the effort.

2 November 2016

Mark suggested a weekend getaway to Lisbon. It will be our first; I hope, the first of many.

3 November 2016

He was manipulative to the end, but it's done. Bye, Tristan! Don't call me, I'll call you.

| **PART THREE** |
BABY, I'M A STAR!

2017

Living one's authentic truth is the zeitgeist of this new era, the truth of the heart and of the mind, composed of perspectives and partial understandings, palimpsestic.

The stories we tell ourselves, at peace with our own versions of the past. Each mind pulsates to a narrative of its own construction, but who is left to arbitrate what actually happened?

*

Tristan was haunted by the sound of Seb's keys scraping across the floorboards as he pushed open the door, life as he knew it at an end.

He dragged his body around, functioning but not, stunned. He carried the weight of Seb's departure with him always; the loss of his future, gone in a second but also never really there. The humiliation ravaged his mind; the getaway bag in the hallway, the matter of fact delivery, the recitation of a memorised script.

Its brutality unhinged him.

He lived for the one second gap between waking and his mind remembering.

How was any of this even possible?

Yet here he was, at his nadir.

Dominick and Toby listened to his examinations and re-examinations of what had occurred. He questioned every decision he had made. He cursed his education and those who trained his mind. What use was any of it if this could happen?

"I think he's living nearby," Tristan told them. They were seated around Toby's kitchen table, the remains of a roasted chicken centred before them. They gathered here every Tuesday evening.

Dominick had moved in almost a year ago, accelerating through his youth in favour of walks on the beach and candlelit dinners, and since then he had quietly but firmly asserted himself on the situation and the place. Tristan was pleased for them, and he enjoyed experiencing the parts of their life they chose to share with him, but he envied them all the parts they did not, and the exuberance of their life made him mourn all he had lost.

Dominick put down his fork and reached for the stem of his wine glass, exposing the long, bony fingers which reminded Tristan of ET.

"Are you sure?" he asked him.

"He walked right past me."

Dominick slowly swallowed his wine as he assessed the extent of Tristan's distress. He found his mood difficult to anticipate.

"Did you speak to him?"

"No. He was with someone. One of his boyfriends, presumably. I was too shocked to speak. I couldn't even look."

Seb's brazenness offended him. The capacity to live well, knowing what he had done, that was offensive, too.

"I spend every hour thinking about him, and he doesn't even care, he's walking down the middle of the street with his head held high." Tristan's voice cracked. "How could someone even do that?"

The question is always why; part of us forever remains the child seeking an explanation, incredulous that, eventually, the only possible answer is 'just because'.

Tristan poured more wine into his glass. "I need to get out of that apartment. I'm going to die if I stay there." The rooms still smelled of him. He could hear the echo of Seb's thoughts in them.

Toby excused himself, pleading pressure of work. It had been like this for months, the same analysis on loop, and it was difficult to witness. The abundance of his love, rejected out of hand, surplus.

Tristan swirled the liquid in his glass, watching it cling to the sides. He lingered. He didn't want to leave.

*

Toby was a law firm partner of two years standing and there was no financial quarter between his accession and now in which he was operating at anything other than a definitive net loss. He thought the dynamic would change when he was made up, but it was always the same dynamic, it was always a transaction in which one person had power and the other did not, in which someone wanted something and someone else had to decide whether to give it to them.

He knew the work backwards. He knew what to do, and when to do it, and how. He knew the time it would take and the cost, and he knew which strategies to apply to expedite as much of the process as possible, and he knew which bits to do himself and how to staff the rest of it. He knew the likely outcomes, and the probabilities of each. He knew all of it so well, he was no longer curious about it. Yet every time he answered the phone, or opened an email, he was surprised it didn't lead to catastrophe.

He was angry about it, and he took it out on his staff, adopting an abrasive style. His bluntness helped cement his reputation as a slender bruiser, pugnacious and ready for battle. There were enough people who wanted to work for him, but only the most bullish survived. People thought he was difficult, and he found it was not an unhelpful reputation, feared by his colleagues for his tenacity, and for his professional prowess.

Last week, Toby passed out on the bathroom floor, smashing the right side of his face on the cast iron tub as he fell. He knew as soon as he regained consciousness his face would bruise, and it did, but none of his colleagues asked of the injury, and it made him wonder how much they knew.

Dominick professed his support, but also, he despaired. It frustrated him.

"I know you're trying," Dominick told him. "I just wish you didn't need to try. I wish this wasn't something you had to fight against so hard."

He wished Toby could be happy with what they had, or at least spend less time finding ways to keep himself miserable.

*

Tristan's grief became obsessional. If only Seb could witness his desolation, he would return.

And what was the life which awaited Seb if he did not? After this betrayal, another, then another still, the flotsam of past lives ever longer. He would, surely, betray the man for whom Tristan was betrayed.

They became adults together when their lives were still in their opening bars. Never again could he love someone he had come to know like that.

It was unthinkable. The man next to whom he slept every night for all those years, dismissing him as collateral damage. And for what? A life of callousness, making a fool of everyone unfortunate enough to love him, thrusting himself into perpetual renewals.

Oh, Seb knows what he has done, Tristan said to himself; he knows the injustice of it, and its horror, and its impact, that was why he chose to stay away.

It was unfathomable, beyond the orbit of anything Tristan had ever known to be true. How had he come to love a person like that?

"I know it's an odd decision," Seb had said, his tone defiant. "But it is my decision to make. I know it is selfish." There was a righteousness in the way he spoke that night, Tristan could hear it now.

How satisfying it would be to demonise him and all the decisions he had made which had brought them to this point, yet Seb's decision to leave was part of him, and Tristan loved every part of him still.

He missed him.

"He is not worth it," Toby told him. "He is who he is, and he wants what he wants. A man is more than his mistakes."

"Don't you get it?" Tristan was offended by Toby's even-handedness, and by his failure to recognise the depth of his distress.

"You could never be quite sure what he was thinking, I suppose. He went out of his way never to talk about himself. He was an 'issues' guy."

Toby was summoned to London to explain his financials. When the moment came, he was surprised, but not. He listened and played for time. He thought of them as dreamcatchers, taking his dreams and making a business out of them.

He called Freddie and asked to see him.

"Sure, come to the office."

Freddie was still on the treadmill when he arrived—Freddie liked to run, said nothing could beat the feeling, that only when he was running could he see the world in all its complexity, and knew it was there for the taking, and that his role in it was unique and beautiful—so an improbably young, improbably good-looking bond trader showed him into Freddie's office to wait. He was a decade younger than Toby, but spoke to him in a tone which conveyed an unshakeable self-regard: *all that you are, all that you value, it means nothing to me.*

Freddie had learned how to use eye contact as a threat, that was the first thing Toby noticed when he entered the room. He liked seeing Freddie in this setting. He was so capable, and cold.

"I'll come straight to the point," he began, as Freddie sat down at his desk. "You have to give me some work. Anything. I'm begging you."

"Of course," Freddie replied, almost absent-mindedly, as he scanned the papers before him. "I'll send something over. I was meaning to; I would have anyway. Wolves at the door, are they?"

"Something like that."

Freddie clasped his hands together, as though about to pray, then looked up.

"You could have just asked. You didn't have to get on your knees. I can't bear it when a man begs."

"I'm not begging, as such."

"You just said 'I'm begging you'."

"It's a turn of phrase."

"Even so."

Freddie had worked at the hedge fund for the past seven years and, although he wasn't particularly alpha in his outlook, he did reasonably well; he was good with numbers and his presence was much sought after because of his looks and quietly reassuring aura. But he survived because a cold ruthlessness ran through him; he saw his life as a quest to find the critical cogs at the centre of the machine, which no one else could see were vital to the process. Most of the time, he felt he was playing a game he couldn't lose. He used the language of war and the metaphors of sport and praised working round the clock. He had a sureness about him, a certainty which was more than skin deep. He could be cruel, too. He picked on the weakest and humiliated them in meetings; extrapolating utter incompetence from a carelessly used word. He did it again and again and again and he was rewarded for it, told he had killer instinct.

"Are you alright, though?" he asked Toby.

"I'm fine."

"You look like you've wept." That bloody word, he told himself as he said it. Mrs. Green, that *woman*.

"I'm not sleeping that well. It makes my eyes puffy."

Freddie looked at him suspiciously.

"I cried on the plane, actually. Watching *Philadelphia*."

"Fair enough," Freddie replied. "You're pretty much just a deadly disease from being that guy."

An intern opened the door to Freddie's office and started to walk towards him.

"Get out," he told her. She apologised.

"Was that really necessary?" Toby asked him.

"It doesn't matter. She's useless." Freddie collected his thoughts. "You know, Toby, when people witness an accident, they're just passers-by or whatever, and they say afterwards, 'I helped them as best I could,' and they explain what they did to tend to the injured—I mean, who in hell knows what they did, maybe they applied a compress or whatever, maybe a tourniquet, I mean, they probably made the situation worse—and they're welling up as they recall the horror of it all and you just know they want all the praise that's going for—being the good Samaritan, I guess. Well, they have their reasons. But they are damaged by what they have seen, psychologically. That's why I'm not one of those people who stops to help. If that makes me a bad person, so be it." He stood up. "What you need to do, Toby, is learn to keep on walking."

It was only when Freddie deposited Toby into the lift to lower him back to street level that Toby realised there had been no suggestion of getting lunch.

He boarded a train at King's Cross to take him back to Edinburgh. He was glad to leave. He never had found a way of feeling at ease in London, and he hated himself for it. Edinburgh was a construct of his mind; it was a concept, an adjunct of an idea. It was a receptacle for the stories he had told himself.

The thought of home, and Dominick there waiting for him, gave relief to his mind. But, also, he knew. Home, another item in a long list of items which could be taken away from him, suddenly, brutally, by means he had failed to anticipate, blindsided.

*

Tristan could not outrun all the fears metastasising inside him. The meanings of his life, he suddenly understood, were only an illusion; none of his stabilities were true.

Seb was gone. He would never return.

There was so much of him Tristan had never known. He saw it now: how much Seb had kept from him, how careful he had been with the information he chose to reveal; two-faced, secretive.

How sparse and thin Tristan's knowledge of him was. He had projected so many of his idealisations onto him. But he knew nothing, really, of his character, or of how he had been raised, or if others held him in esteem.

The evidence of his manipulations.

Yet still, he was trapped, and Seb was free.

Was this the enduring humiliation awaiting him? Whole years of his life lost to Seb's secret pathways?

How to rid himself of the delusions still in his heart.

At the limits of his endurance, and still the pain grew.

He looked for a way out.

*

Toby was filling in a form which asked him to specify whether he felt suicidal, yes or no. He didn't want to admit to it in writing; once you started down that path, who knew where you would end up. He contemplated declining to answer but feared the negative inference.

He placed a large cross in the no box, then realised it was much too big. It was far bigger than any of the other crosses. Its lack of proportion drew attention to itself; it would give him away. He ripped up the form and asked for another, binning his first attempt as he made his way back to the sofa.

He started again, making good progress onto the second page, before realising how easily someone could piece back together the neat squares he had discarded. He retrieved them from the wastepaper basket, requested a black marker pen, found the square with the incriminating cross, and struck it out with satisfying thick black lines.

He allowed himself the briefest moment of pleasure before he realised. The ink! What conspiracies it would seduce in the mind of the reasonable man! The hell of our articulations!

He got down on his knees and set to work on the other pieces.

A male voice called his name.

He turned around and looked up.

"Do you want to bring the wastepaper basket with you?"

They climbed the stairs, Toby first, his psychiatrist second, the pile of the carpet cushioning their steps.

Seated facing a window, Toby crossed his legs, then uncrossed them and wondered what to do with his hands.

He looked around and felt the urge to fill the silence.

"You were recommended," he said, hearing the strain in his voice.

"That is always nice to hear." The psychiatrist pulled a lever which tilted his chair towards the desk. "Is my having been recommended important to you?"

"I don't want someone mediocre."

The psychiatrist looked at him over the brim of his spectacles and started writing in his file in handwriting which, Toby assumed, was deliberately difficult to read. Toby listened to the scratch of the nib.

"Did you fill in the form?"

Toby glanced at the ink-stained fingers on his left hand.

"Never mind. What happened to your hand?"

"This?" Toby asked, pointing to the ink stain.

"I meant the other one."

"Oh."

He took one step at a time, making a gradual descent, feeling the usual unease.

*

Tristan read biographies, consoled by the complexity of other people's lives. He read autobiographies, too, but read between the lines, hunting for gaps, and short chapters about big events. He was surprised by just how unsentimental people could be. He turned to novels for a more reliable narrative.

It was a bare existence, but it did at least feel like existence.

The months continued to pass, month after month after month.

In time, he realised the same negative version of the story was keeping him in victimhood. And in time, he remembered he had a degree of control over how he chose to live.

What a devastation it had been to invest all his hopes and all his dreams in the whims of another. Why terrorise himself with the belief that, without Seb, he could not live?

He identified what he could, in fact, fix.

His mind alternated between the need for action, to do something, anything, and to do it quickly, and the realisation that what he actually needed was whole days to sit and think, for weeks to pass without doing anything very much at all.

When he realised he was about to toss his old life aside, he cried. Not even Seb had made him cry. He had been too shocked to cry then and, after the shock had passed, tears seemed rather beside the point.

"What do you think George Michael would do?" his psychoanalyst asked, and they were off, cantering through the chapters of his life!

Toby was here because Dominick wanted him to voice more of his fears. If he said them out loud, thought Dominick, it would lessen their hold on him.

"It's the easiest thing in the world, Toby, to live like everyone else," she told him. "The conventions have failed you, Toby, as they do all of us, eventually. You might want to ask yourself why they continue to have such hold over you."

He joined a book club, tried a running club, started singing in a chorus. He tried yoga.

"What about contacting some old friends you want to welcome back into your life?" suggested Dominick.

As an idea, it wasn't his worst, so Toby sent off the messages, each carefully crafted and personalised, and the replies came in. No one said no. But no one really said yes, either. Some of the people invited him to an event they already had planned, and to which others had already been invited. The coded message, as Toby interpreted it, was: we like to socialise in bulk, we like to see as many people as possible in as short a space of time as possible, we like to tick people off the list. Others were taking bookings for five weeks on Friday; all other slots were booked.

He watched films. He enjoyed shutting out the light, the certainty of what the next two hours would bring, your phone shut off and the outside world kept reassuringly at arm's length.

Every night Toby returned home to discover Dominick there still, and he was surprised, and grateful. He started lying, camouflaging his mood so Dominick would not leave.

He promised himself each hour would contain at least one moment of joy, no matter how small.

Each night, he asked himself, 'Is this what it feels like to be free?'.

*

Tristan wanted his channel to represent a mood and a period and a problem.

"Turning your life on its head like this, it means you're still dancing to his tune," Toby told him.

Not so, thought Tristan. He didn't want his old life back. He was embarked on a major transition, and the terror he felt about it reassured him. It's not real change if at first it does not terrify you.

Toby meant well, but what he had to offer wasn't what Tristan wanted to hear and Tristan, for his part, didn't want to say much about it to Toby at all. They used to agree how to live, and they had lived parallel lives for years, but now they were at an impasse, each thinking the other a fool.

"The thing is," Dominick explained to him, "every time you talk about how much happier you are now, all Toby hears is an attack on the choices he made."

"Doesn't that mean he's not sure he made the right choices?"

"It's not that. He just hasn't realised that what he loves leaves you cold."

Five weeks had passed, and Tristan hadn't done any of the things he now knew would have to be done in order to launch himself as a credible proposition. There was no channel, no content, just the ego required to think he could make it. And there was the issue of how to monetise a brand which didn't yet exist.

But what he did have was an idea. It wasn't necessarily original, but it was specific to him because it was about him, he was at the very centre of it, and it felt authentic in a way nothing else had for a long time. It was an idea which was multi-faceted, he could see it from all its angles, he could walk towards it as if it were a shape on a landscape he had known all his life. He knew too much about it to state what it was, and when he spoke about it, he could feel the resistance.

"What's it about, exactly?" Toby asked him. "The channel."

Tristan paused. "It's hard to say."

"It sounds like you don't yet have a coherent concept. You need to figure out what it is, then find a way to express it in no more than two sentences. That way, people will know you are serious."

"Yes," Tristan replied.

"I mean it, though. If this is what you really want, you must get on with it. There's a window of opportunity for these things. I'm just saying you don't want to miss out. I support you, though. If it doesn't work out, you can always come back. It wasn't all bad."

Tristan worked in coffee shops, writing down ideas, broad brush strokes hinting at what he might want to say. He centred his experience, uncompromisingly, on himself. It was his story, but it was also a version of a story most people knew. He included every stray thought and calculated how much recording time he would allocate to each. Twenty minutes on messaging etiquette. Ten minutes on why people with no capital believe in capitalism. Two hours on running your own race. Two minutes on learning to say no. As long as was necessary on how to be alone, and what it feels like to be left behind. He wanted people to feel personally addressed. He filled an A4 pad with text and connective arrows. It was helpful, but it was also too much. He realised it was less about the ideas than about the process of asserting himself over them.

When he pressed record, he was in the moment, but he was also looking down at himself wondering why it had taken him so long when this is how it should always have been.

| PART FOUR |
A WRECKONING

Late 2017

1

Late afternoon. Three hours and counting.

Dinner parties were difficult for Toby, but there were only so many dishes Dominick could make for two, so every so often he insisted. It took its toll.

His palms started sweating, and his acne spread from under his chin, onto his cheeks and up into his forehead. Dominick told him he was ridiculous.

"These people are your friends! They have your back, they're on your side!"

Were they, though? How ill-equipped we are for each other, the eurhythmics of all there is still to know, and all we might yet be.

His routine disturbed, instead he had to hustle, cleaning and preparing and panic-buying, and by the time the apartment was ready, and the food was ready and they, in theory, were ready, at the exact moment, in other words, which gave Dominick the greatest pleasure—seeing everything in its place, ready for a gathering, its beauty not yet disturbed by the people for whom it was intended—that was when Toby felt lightheaded with fear.

Freddie knocked loudly on the door; even the sound of his knuckles on the glass-panelling conveyed his exuberance. Thicker of waist since Toby last saw him, which wasn't even that long ago, he looked well, and thoroughly in control.

"New hair product?" Toby asked, grasping for anything. Freddie's hair, he thought, had been lacquered in pomade.

"Huh?"

Cordelia stood behind him, darkly imposing in a full-length navy dress. Freddie stood aside, his social manners apposite as always, and as she sashayed past his patch-pocketed navy blazer, their bodies for the briefest moment fused into one.

Toby and Cordelia bear-hugged, and each put a hand on the other's back as they walked along a hallway not quite wide enough for a two-step.

"Postmodernism always was a self-defeating formulation," Dominick told them as he poured the wine. "It's not a theory, it's a free for all. Anything goes. There's nothing really there to grab onto and believe."

Igor sipped his wine as he listened to Dominick covering old ground.

"It's no good, for example, telling people 'The System' doesn't exist, because it does, and it's here, and we're living in it."

Igor and Toby exchanged looks.

"Well, sounds like it's coming along nicely," Igor commented.

From the far end of the kitchen came the opening notes of an Ellington playlist.

"Anyway," said Dominick. "Toby disapproves."

"I'm supportive," Toby protested. "I mean, I love a meta mutiny as much as the next guy. I'm just saying I used to think all of that as well, when I was twenty-three."

"The age card," replied Dominick. "Really?"

"Oh, come on! Be fair. It was a joke."

Freddie's consumption on the trading circuit was of some repute, and he applied the same diligence off-duty. His naval constitution had no time for hangovers, and, inspired by the eighties formula for getting ahead, he made do with very little sleep, running his course between the extremities. During the dinner, he didn't waste a drop of his eleven goblets of wine, and his licentiousness rose to the occasion when the bittersweet Amari was proffered as an aid to his digestion.

Toby felt his despair slinking around in the hinterland. It was the enemy within, the saboteur, signalling its intent, hinting at the ferocity of its grip. The energy it took to stop it consuming everything in its path, it exhausted him. 'Confide in me' had its limits; after a point, the pool of people who wanted to know diminished until all you had were the people duty bound to keep on listening. Not that there was much to say. Medication didn't work, talking about it didn't work, throwing money at it didn't work, so it was on him to make himself better: more exercise, more healthy eating, more manifestation of the positive, more of nothing very much at all. The way to happiness, it seemed, involved forsaking everything that used to make you happy and then to make a virtue of feeling bereft. So, it was the same as it always had been, but worse, because now there was less hope it would ever be better.

Tristan drifted off, opened the doors which led out into the garden, glad of the air and of the chance to stare out into the night.

Cordelia looked on, salamander in hand. "Still pining for the boy, then. No one can accuse him of not being loyal to his suffering."

"Shut up, Cordelia," said Toby.

"Toby, it's been years. His sadness is becoming—terminal."

"It was first love. Of course, its dimensions are out of all proportion. He's still stunned by its afterglow." Cordelia did not approve of the indulgence of it, its weakening sensibilities. "It will take as long as it takes," Toby added.

She made her noise of exasperation again, a glottal exhalation. "Torn to pieces by a boy! I mean, I met him, and I am at a loss to understand what all the fuss is about."

*

Tristan winced at Toby's suggestion of a top-up.

"There's only so much pop I can drink before my gullet requires something more savage."

They relocated to the living room, just the two of them, the voices next door loud and lively. Tristan requested a Negroni and Toby mixed it, as well as a gin martini, for himself.

"We'll have to drink them in here," he told Tristan. "Dominick doesn't like me drinking undiluted gin."

"A gin martini *is* diluted."

"Apparently vermouth doesn't count."

They leafed through Toby's record collection, commenting on the most credible purchases (Dylan, Bush, Roux) and the ones Toby used to hide (Cher, Kylie, Gaga).

"I used to order them alphabetically," Toby explained, "then chronologically, then by genre, but now they're in any old order and I quite like it that way. You never know what you might find."

Toby couldn't remember the last time he'd played any of them, he noted silently, as he lit the candles on either side of the mantlepiece and adjusted the books on the alcove shelves, lining up the spines. He nudged the sofa back into position and sat down to finish his drink. His gloom deepening, he resolved to see the night through. The valour of perseverance would make him feel good about himself tomorrow.

"Now this, I love!" Tristan was clutching *Captain Fantastic* and looking at the B-side. "Remember we used to dance to this in the office."

"You remember that?"

Tristan gave him a look which dismayed at the possibility either of them could ever forget.

"Let's put it on."

*

"Are you just going to stand there?" asked Dominick.

"I have to stand somewhere," replied Toby, Tristan slinking in behind him.

"We need mood music."

Toby picked Lester Young, poured out a jug of iced water, placed it on the table, dimmed the lights.

Cordelia offered to help with service, but Dominick declined, dubious of her capacity to plate with finesse. He placed hunks of halibut into the centre of each bowl, then spooned quantities of broth over and around. He clattered the mussels into a colander, reserving some of their liquor, and bejewelled each plate with two of the plumpest specimens, then realised three looked better.

"It's really good, Dominick," Tristan said of it, done after three mouthfuls. His teeth were undergoing expensive dentistry and his mouth was aflame.

Freddie, holding his cutlery the wrong way around—an error of childhood corrected too late to reverse the habit—cut through the flesh of the halibut, gripping his knife like someone was about to steal it from him. Igor used only his fork, pressing down on the fish until it flaked into edible morsels. Toby rushed through his, bored of identifying each ingredient, bored of eating mindfully, bored even of that nasty little word.

Igor reached over him for the breadbasket.

It had occurred to Toby halfway through his second gin martini there would be scope for unnoticed excess, so he excused himself, opened another bottle of White Burgundy, decanted it, and poured as much of it as he decently could into his glass, drank that with his back turned to the others and poured himself another, before returning to the table.

The others talked.

The monomaniac strength of the suppressed thought! The abyss of battle, the persistence of the damned!

Toby drank another three glasses in quick succession.

Dominick stood up, began gathering in the plates. Tristan was embarrassed by his leftovers.

"I'm sorry," he said.

"Don't be."

He did look in pain. When he laughed, all Dominick could see was steel.

The others said it was so good Dominick should have been a chef.

"There's still time," Toby suggested.

"But a chef, though? We'd never see each other. I'd have to work nights."

Toby said it wasn't the nature of the job which appealed to him so much as the concept of having a job. "You don't want to be a student for the rest of your life."

"I might. What you mean is you don't want me to be a student for the rest of *your* life."

Toby raised his arms to his sky in proclamation. "Finally, he understands!"

At the heart of Toby's mistrust was a plea for purity. We all make liars of each other, he knew, but the politeness of it angered him; the code, the surface skating, talking and talking and talking, just words.

He could have gone to bed. He could have excused himself to change the music and collapsed on the sofa, out for the count. Yes, that's what he should have done. But instead, he stayed.

Why were they talking so loudly? Loudly and full of gestures, looping the conversation back to themselves, hearing only the words which served as a steppingstone back to what they wanted to say.

"I'm not saying it's a key factor, but it is important."

"There are historically specific reasons for that."

"I've worked with him twice now. He's good, but hardly a leader in waiting."

Clunking along, the incessance of their observations.

Toby scraped back his chair, stood up unsteadily, and told them to leave.

"Get out! Get out of my house!"

Dominick looked at him, astonished. Toby was surprised, too, but on some level, what he felt was relief.

"Can I at least finish my wine?" Freddie asked. "I just poured it."

Toby took the glass out of his hand and tossed its contents onto him.

"There we are," said Toby, a smile on his face. "It's finished now. That's your cue to fuck off."

Freddie looked down at the flourishing stain on his shirt and clenched his right fist.

Toby noted with satisfaction how little provocation Freddie required.

So it was left to Cordelia, who channelled as much of her mother's social grace she could muster; she didn't want Toby to feel bad.

"It's late," she said. "We should be going."

"Well, if you'd been on time."

"We arrived two minutes after eight," Igor protested. "How much more prompt do you need people to be?"

"No. You're on time, or you're not. Late, or not. You're reliable, or you're not. Either you're someone upon whom I can depend, or you're not. And you, it seems, are not."

"Really?" Dominick said, his voice somewhere between fury and despair. "Is this how you want the night to end? It was going so well. You were doing so well."

Toby stared at him. "Don't patronise me."

"Don't even start, Toby. I just can't."

As they all made their way along the path and onto the pavement, Toby slammed the front door shut and could have sworn he heard laughter.

He made himself another gin martini, dispensing with the shaker, drank it, poured some Malbec, drank that, poured another. Aloneness, now he had it in his grasp, wasn't the complete solution he hoped it might be. And it hadn't occurred to him Dominick would leave too. That part of it, that was— unforeseen. The audacity of it, its insufferability, it was a betrayal he would not let stand.

Toby threw his glass at the wall. It shattered messily, and Malbec coated the paint and the floor in vermillion droplets.

He walked into the master bedroom, closed the door, undressed, and sat on his corner of the bed, running his fingers over the hospital-cornered bedsheets. It was quiet now. He reached into the drawer of his bedside table and was calm. What he felt was valid, and it was beautiful.

2

Toby was pronounced dead at eleven thirty-four on Sunday morning, although the paramedic team assumed he had been without life for at least two or so hours before that, but there was no way to be sure, and so the formal time of death was the moment they looked for a pulse and found none.

Dominick discovered the situation—its intimacy and its fury—about two hours after he returned home, sleep-deprived and still angry.

At first, he couldn't bear to enter their bedroom, knowing Toby would be in there, and when he did eventually, he assumed Toby was ignoring him. He had done it before, many times. He said, afterwards, Toby looked like he was asleep, but all he meant by that was he was under the covers and all he could see was his hair.

He didn't tell people the last part, nor did he tell people of his work fixing what Toby had trashed. If he'd spent less time scrubbing wine off the hallway floor, would he have found him sooner?

He assumed Toby had hurled it out of spite.

Dominick remembered demanding of him: "Get up. Come and look at what you have done."

He remembered the absence of a reply. But even that wasn't unusual. Instinctively he was manipulative.

Dominick wasn't sure anyone told him Toby was dead. He would come to feel a cold hatred towards them for that. It became apparent from the circumstances: the hush in the room, the absence of activity, the ambulance workers no longer trying to pummel Toby into life, the packing up of the machinery, of the equipment. Dominick recalled thanking them for their efforts. He might even have offered them tea. There was a teapot on the kitchen counter, so one of them might even have said yes.

Two police officers seated themselves on the sofa opposite the fireplace. Dominick saw his surprise reflected in the way they looked at him. He had shown them in, but he didn't remember, and they asked their questions, alternating between sympathy and suspicion. Dominick felt sorry for them. Their uniforms looked itchy and uncomfortable, and their phraseology was clumsy. But there was an earnestness about them; they were trying their best. Later, Dominick would wonder why he made it easy for them, why it never occurred to him that sometimes it is acceptable not to smile.

"I don't think he acted with intention."

"Are you asking us to consider his passing death by misadventure?"

When they eventually left, not totally convinced Dominick hadn't force-fed him the pills, he bolted the door and called Tristan, the rules of what was thinkable forever changed.

*

It is the age of the individual, our mortality the only tie which binds; the hurdle which cannot be overcome.

Tristan and Igor made their way through the silent lamentations of the cemetery. The church continued the good

118

fight, but even the vandalism was in a state of decay, and the long-term trajectory was clear: fallen gravestones, the grass wild, the atrophy of what once was grand, the earth giving way.

It didn't look as if anyone was taking care of anything anymore.

Toby's father greeted them at the door, charmless, and reserved to the point of remote. The young lawyers next in line were sad, but also excited about their revised path to partnership in light of Toby vacating his spot. "What a great guy! I had no idea he was suicide ideated," said one of them, surely lying.

They entered the already full church and made their way down the aisle in search of seating. No one had thought to reserve the front rows, so the arrangements were haphazard: friends before family, pallbearers squeezed next to third cousins twice removed, Dominick on the end of the sixth row. Tristan and Igor found Freddie, and Cordelia next to him. The atmosphere was pulled tight; the death of the young, the life half-lived.

The tears wept by the woman in the Chanel suit in the row behind them reached a hysteria disproportionate to having met Toby but once, and, even then, only as a child.

The minister took his position in the pulpit, turned on the reading light, adjusted the microphone.

> *"We pray for those we love*
> *who now live in a land of shadows,*
> *where the light of memory is dimmed,*
> *where the familiar lies unknown,*
> *where the beloved become as strangers."*

It was just tissue and muscle and bone, Tristan told himself as he looked on at the casket, but still, how claustrophobic he must be in there, trapped.

The minister acknowledged the sadness of the occasion—always that word—and spoke of a Toby Tristan did not recognise. How much of life is really our own? How much of it is devoted to the lives of others, to the ideas of others?

> *"Hold them in your everlasting arms,*
> *and grant to those who care*
> *a strength to serve,*
> *a patience to persevere,*
> *a love to last*
> *and a peace that passes human*
> *understanding."*

He could hold onto him forever, wistfully remembering, but to survive this, Tristan knew he would have to leave him behind. All that Toby had taken with him was lost, and he didn't want to make his way back to it.

The prospect of cancelling Toby from his feelings made his entire body tremble and quake. But he was resolute. Otherwise, he would forever be a subject to its tyranny.

Tristan made his way to the lectern, gripped either side of it, and was silent. When he summoned his voice to address everyone, its pitch was thin, and humbled by loss.

"Right then. Toby, my friend…"

He paused, glanced down, and saw Freddie in a state of dissolution; Cordelia taking his hand as his body rocked back and forth.

"It is possible to live too long," Tristan began, gazing toward the coffin, "to use up more than one's fair share, and who, really, would want to live forever? What a terrible curse!"

There was so much which couldn't be said, which Toby would not have wanted him to say.

"I don't want to think of Toby's life as short or abbreviated. I prefer to think of it as an exemplar of concision."

He heard the echo of his voice reverberate through the speaker system.

"We spent our childhoods together, and many hours of our adulthoods as well. But for Toby, I would not be me."

"His chosen profession was law, and he quickly made his mark as a lawyer; he loved being a partner, and he worked incredibly hard."

Tristan's eyes rested again on the coffin.

"Yet, for all his—practicality, he remained a dreamer, albeit an occasionally melancholic one, and the small number he invited in found a loyal man, a person who was translucent in his affections, and who radiated a luminosity that was as curious as it was occasionally dark."

He looked at Igor, who for the briefest of moments shook his head, signalling no, that was far enough.

"My dear, oversensitive, highly charged, glorious Toby."

It was the same, really, as any of the preceding funerals which had taken place here today already, and of those who were struck by grief or overwhelmed by it, there were as many who were unmoved, their emotions still packaged away neatly in reserve for others. Tristan envied them their ability to return to their lives unscathed. Nor did he care much for their sympathy; sympathy is cheap, everybody is sympathetic until something is required of them.

3

"Is this making anyone feel better?" Freddie asked.

The funeral was weeks ago, yet still they remained in this apartment of death, nursing Dominick, tranquillising themselves with industrial quantities. Sadness was insufficient; the requirement was demonstrable distress. Shared suffering, but each absorbed in his own.

"If you can't be bothered," Cordelia told him, "just go. We'll cope without you. I have before."

When she spoke like this, it made him worry the perspectives of their life together were misaligned.

But he chose to stay: he could see, obliquely, the disgust in resuming their lives, picking up where they left off.

Why pills, he wondered? Such cowardice, just falling asleep. He bristled at the abhorrence of it, and determined to find ways to keep himself angry.

Eventually, Cordelia told him to stop, pitying his distress, how ill-equipped he was as a man.

"He talked about it sometimes," Cordelia told him that evening, their legs entangled on the sofa, the call of the familiar.

"He said what, exactly?" asked Freddie.

"Jumping from the balcony. Wrist razoring. The back-up options."

"Those are just turns of phrase."

"I wonder, though."

"I worked for someone who actually did jump," Freddie added. "Threw himself off the top of the office building. Landed on the pavement outside the front entrance. He was a twat, though."

In the early days, they used to talk about Toby a lot.

"I mean, didn't you know?" He asked her this repeatedly.

"I did not. I'd never met a gay person before."

"But didn't you notice his—reluctance?"

"Not really."

"He could, do the deed?"

"He could."

"And he—did it well?"

"I thought he did, at the time. Retrospectively, I would downgrade him to adequate. He could have—done me a little more."

"God."

"So maybe that was a sign."

"Maybe you thought he was bisexual, I suppose."

"He wasn't, though. At least, not according to his browsing history."

Toby had used her, but still she was not sure if she had allowed herself to be used.

They occupied themselves with practicalities: redecorating the bedroom, appointing a lawyer to represent Dominick's interests over Toby's estate. (They expected a battle, Dominick didn't. They were right.) They contacted Toby's office and ignored their request to collect his personal belongings, binning the flowers they sent. They tried to sort out his finances and were surprised by how much he'd squirrelled away.

"The thing is," Freddie continued, "at least he didn't botch it. At least he didn't wake up depressed and now without working use of his legs. That happens, you know. So at least he was spared that. And at least he died in his own bed."

"Does any of that stuff even matter," asked Igor, genuinely unsure.

"I think it does," Freddie replied, "when there's nothing else left. Then it matters."

*

Toby had dealt Dominick a brutal hand, and they worried for all that was ahead of him.

"Don't do anything drastic, at least not immediately," Tristan advised. "Take it from someone who knows. You think it will set you free. It doesn't."

Dominick did it anyway. He wanted the ashes; they were his and he would have them.

It was eleven o'clock in the morning and Toby's father was red in the face, scotch in hand. He was shorter than Dominick remembered. Not fat, but excessively nourished.

He pretended not to recognise Dominick. They had met briefly, once—a chance encounter on the street—as well as at the funeral, of course, but Dominick introduced himself again, making the point. Toby's father looked out onto his secretary's windowless cubicle and called her a good for nothing shit.

"Why are you here?"

Dominick deepened his voice and adopted an acerbic tone. He'd dealt with plenty of men who liked to call it as they see it. "I want his ashes."

"Do you now."

"He would not want you to have them. You should not have taken them. They were not yours to take."

Dominick sat down on one of the two-barrel chairs facing the desk and crossed his legs.

Toby's father leaned forward, put his elbows on his desk, and clasped his hands. "What I'm going to do is this. I will give you a sum of money, it will be a significant sum of money, it will be enough for you to live on for a considerable amount of time, and you will take the money gladly and, in exchange, you will remove yourself from my son's property, you will leave all of his possessions behind, and you will never present yourself to me, or to my wife, or to anyone else in my family, ever again."

"No."

"No what?"

"No, this is not how it plays out." Dominick looked around. "It must be difficult for you to realise just how little your money is worth."

"Only someone young and poor would say something so incredibly stupid." He thought of depression as a failure of will, a symptom of giving up. He thought his son a coward.

"I am the last link you have to him. I am your access point. Are you not even curious to know what he was like?"

Despite his manner, Dominick was moved by the enormity of what this man in front of him had lost. That he didn't even acknowledge it made the situation somehow worse.

"I know enough already," Toby's father replied. "I don't need you to tell me. Do you think I built all this without knowing what people are?"

Dominick remained silent and stared at him as a therapist would a patient. Toby's father stood up, circled round the Persian rug on which his desk stood, and asked Dominick what he offered in exchange.

"First you offer me money, now you want my terms. This isn't a business transaction."

"Don't be so naïve."

"Toby's ashes are not something to be—traded. It's not commerce, it's ethics. It's—love."

Toby's father walked towards the drinks cabinet to replenish his glass. He poured one for Dominick and passed it to him. "It seems you and my son share the same outlook."

"Wrong again, actually," Dominick told him. Acrimony was key; meekly nodding along would get him nowhere. "Toby was transactional, if you must know. He was convinced everybody wanted something from him."

Toby's father snorted. "Good for him. Maybe he did understand something."

His phone rang. He picked up the receiver and placed it back down without raising it to his ear.

Dominick knocked back all the scotch in his glass and steeled himself against flinching. "Toby never spoke of you as dishonourable. Cantankerous and hard-nosed, yes, but not someone without honour."

*

Dominick worked his way through Toby's indiscriminate hoardings: newspapers, gas bills, lecture notes, shopping receipts, every drawer stuffed full. He didn't know for what he was looking, or where he could find it, but he was determined to piece together the fragments, even if only to dispose of them all, bags of detritus from a former life. Anything which imposed meaning on this mess, anything which offered the composure of control, no matter how illusory. He fought the feeling he could have done more. He looked at every available resource; there was terror in the thought of what he might find, and because so much of it revealed so very little. The paperwork to

126

which he had nailed his life was so unrepresentative of anything very much about him.

How much grieving would be required of him, exactly? Must he remain pinned to the ground, robbed of his lightness, torn to pieces when the blindsiding force of history comes to call? Just because happiness was beyond Toby's attainment, was he required to forsake his own?

Igor was restless, pining for London and his own bed. He calculated when he could escape without causing offence and, when he left, he was satisfied he had done his bit. He had tried to help, but whether he had or not, it was time. The others didn't leave so much as just stopped being around. They had stuff to do, and Dominick learnt there are limits to what even the best of friendships can offer. There is always a home time, another life to be tended and lived. Life carried on, and eventually he would be expected to do the same. Tristan was the last to leave, and the others were quietly grateful.

"Rather him than me," said Freddie.

On the evening of his scheduled departure, Tristan surveyed each of the rooms, checked the fridge was full, made sure the WIFI worked. After two circuits, including a brief excursion outside to check the garden, all that was left was goodbye. They stood in the doorway, as three students filed out of the neighbouring tenement door. Tristan put his arms on Dominick's shoulders and faced him.

"Tristan, don't. I don't think I can."

*

Six weeks later, Cordelia told Freddie she was pregnant.

| PART FIVE |
OXFORD
2005

"It's not that it's bad," Igor began.

Bun-tied hair, the same old pair of skinny black jeans, his gown hanging on the door peg, bolstering his superstar credentials. They were sitting in an attic room above the President's Lodgings, and light was streaming in through the pointy little windows facing Broad Street.

"No, it's not bad, as such," he continued. "The problem— well, the problem." Igor stopped. "Sorry, could you just move to the right a bit? The sun is bouncing off your glasses and blinding me."

"Your right or my right?"

"Either."

Mark shuffled left, his left, scraping the armchair along the floor with his chequerboard shoes. He wore a dark blue linen shirt with disdain.

"Better?"

"Sorry, no. Try the other way."

"I could just take them off."

"Your glasses? No, don't do that."

Mark scraped right, his right. "Better now?"

"Better."

Igor collected his thoughts.

"The problem, well, the problem is it's boring. Beyond tedious, actually." He tried to gauge Mark's reaction, but all he could see were red dots. "It's boring to read, so it must have been boring to write."

Mark just sat there, looking vacant, absent-mindedly poking at the titanium bolt through his left eyebrow. His stubble disguised the acne bumps raging underneath.

"Tell me you were bored when you wrote it!"

Mark nodded, unsure of Igor's heading.

"Thank God. I mean, can you imagine if you weren't! Then we really would be fucked." Igor flicked through the pages and yawned. "I mean, really, unspeakably dull."

He looked at the perching birds on the chestnut tree as he slipped off his shoes and hoisted his feet onto the chair. The plumage of the finches caught his eye.

"So…"

"So," Mark replied.

"Where were we, again? Forgive me."

"You were talking about boredom."

"Yes," said Igor, trying to remember the cause of it, precisely. "Take your first paragraph, for example. You use all nineteen sentences of it to express iterations of what seems to be the Husserlian line that 'knowledge'—by which you presumably mean 'meaning'—is fixed, irrespective of how it is expressed, and fair enough, I mean, that is a position one can adopt, so I read on, excited about the journey, but by the time I've read all the way to the bottom of page three, it turns out you don't have all that much to say about Husserl, and eventually you tire of him altogether, so I turn the page wondering what's next, and all of a sudden you announce that 'Reason' is where it's at, so you co-opt the Hegelian principle and tell me 'Reason' is the concept of all concepts, is beyond rational scrutiny, and so on and so forth, so now I'm thinking, well, that as a concept is fair enough as well, but what connects any of these concepts to the question posed?"

Mark shifted in his seat.

"I intended to follow the pre-Socratean argument about 'Being'."

"Go on."

"We will never identify the exact characteristics of 'Being' because we are a product of it and so we can never step out of it."

"So, it's not Husserl and it's not Hegel, it's Heidegger. We're going to run out of philosophers whose surnames begin with 'H'."

Igor leafed through the remaining pages.

"Then, at page seven, after a footnoted detour to have a go at the logo-centrists—which, in any another context, I would have quite enjoyed—you abandon all this stuff about 'knowledge' and 'meaning' and 'Reason' and—sorry, what was the other one, the one you just said?"

"'Being'."

"Yes, so you abandon all of them and instead devote your remaining words to Foucault and why there is no such thing as human nature." Igor looked down and noticed the ring he was wearing on the middle finger of his right hand made his skin look swollen. "So, all in all, quite the turbulent journey."

Igor offered him a Lucky Strike, took another for himself, and lit both as Mark opened the window.

They smoked in silence as tourists congregated around the entrance gates.

"Returning to our journey through the 'Hs'," Igor said eventually. "Maybe you were too quick to abandon Hegel."

Mark looked at him blankly.

"*Absolute Spirit?*" Still nothing. "This thing you say you believe in; you conceive of it as completely outside all other reality to the point it cannot be known or spoken. Hegel's *Absolute* can be known."

Mark wrote down *'Absolute Spirit'* on the back of page seven.

"Or try Nietzsche," Igor suggested, scratching next to the lotus flower tattooed onto the bottom of his left leg. "He's with you on the fallacy of objective reality, but your reasonings are very different, so you need to get to grips with him, too."

Mark asked if that was spelled with a 'z'. "Just kidding," he added.

Igor stubbed out his cigarette. He thought Mark was capable, and his rebellion seemed less mainstream than most. Still, if he wanted to play at this level, if this part of it didn't come easily, what was the point?

"Same time tomorrow?"

"What should I write for it?" asked Mark.

"Nothing, really. I don't think I could take it. Just pick a book by Hegel, or by Nietzsche I suppose, either will do, read it, and then we'll talk about it."

"Any book?"

"Any book."

He could only take him so far along the path before he was basically doing it for him.

*

Toby was in the library sitting in his usual spot: the aisle seat three rows in on the right-hand side, his back to the door. Of late, he had been taking up two spaces, surrounded by his folders, and his post-it notes, and the pages and pages of ideas he wrote down using a Parker fountain pen, the nib gnarled into the shape his hand required to scrawl almost legible words. It was against the rules, technically, reserving a space for himself like this, and using the one next to it as well was a further infringement, but the librarian liked him and chose to overlook it. He liked her too; the first time they met, she loaned him a book from her private collection and told him she didn't like it here at first, either.

He heard the click of the door lock and turned to see one of the good-looking boys from the year below, and the girl with whom he spent most of his time. They muted their laughter as they hurried past him and down the stairwell to the lower library. But for them, he had the library to himself.

It was mid-evening and he had spent most of the day in bed, woken periodically by the communal door outside his room slamming shut. He'd risen as the sun was setting and showered in a thickly grimed cubicle using a little bottle of bodywash he'd found languishing at the bottom of one of his desk drawers.

He was reviewing yesterday's work, and he had a clear plan in his mind of what he wanted to read tonight and how he thought it would shape his argument. It was satisfying to read back what he had written, to agree with most of it, or at least the direction it was taking, and to find his thoughts reflected back at him. He told himself this was the way out of his feelings, that the answers had been here all along, that all he had to do was look. He sprayed three squirts of a herbal remedy onto his tongue and settled down into the task. Sixty pages in and his notepad filling up nicely, he was lost in thought about moral equivocation, transported into a world which seemed manageable; it only existed to the extent he cared to read the words on the page and then think about them.

He hadn't eaten. Sometimes, he ate something from the kebab van parked outside the gates; sometimes Cordelia cooked for him. Usually, he just waited until he could bear the hunger no longer and then grabbed the first thing available, eating it quickly and not especially aware of what it was. Tonight, he worked on, hungry but not hungry enough to do anything about it.

At just gone midnight, Igor entered the library, dressed in iterations of black and smelling of Lucky Strikes, his long curly brown hair sticking out of the hoodie covering his head. He acknowledged Toby—was that a Manchester accent, Toby wondered—and started climbing the narrow wooden stairwell up to the mezzanine. Toby could hear the slouch in his footsteps.

At three am, Toby departed, Igor apparently still up there.

He located his bike and cycled down to the High Street, turned left on Aldgate and built-up speed on his way to Cowley's terraced rows, where Cordelia lived in a house share. He didn't know the address; actually, he struggled even to remember what the house looked like. He certainly couldn't describe it, but it was a straightforward journey, and he knew the route by heart. She was already in bed when he arrived, but he didn't have a key and he didn't want to ring the buzzer—he was already unpopular with her housemates, there was no point in making it worse—so he rang her phone three times, one of those small Nokias with the impossibly hard buttons, and on the third attempt, she answered.

"You said you would be here for dinner," she remonstrated with him, her face full of sleep.

"No, I didn't."

They walked up the stairs to the attic bedroom and settled into her single bed.

*

It was a crisp May morning, and the sun's coruscating rays danced on the speared tips atop the tall blue gates. Toby looked on from the opposite side of Broad Street, rummaging around his backpack for his bike lock, then wheeled the bike across the street and through the college entrance, which, as he noticed every time he walked through it, was more bungalow than fortress. He hadn't thought to check before he applied and now, when he looked at the other colleges, he envied their sturdy frontage. The friendlier of the porters acknowledged him as he passed the open window, as the less friendly one stuffed pigeonholes with TV licensing demands and library fines. Toby walked on.

He bought breakfast in hall and asked the college president for a section of one of the eight papers spread out next to his boiled egg.

"I was rather planning on reading them all," he replied.

Toby blushed and retreated to the other side of the hall, where he ate alone, listening in on the lycra-clad rowers teasing each other about acting gay. Toby found it difficult not to look. One of the better-looking ones acknowledged him from afar, told him to take it easy as he walked out.

He read all morning in the library, his hands on his temples, using his elbows to keep the books open without breaking their spines, then bought coffee for the people around him, taking the cups past the no drinks sign as the fellows in the Danson Room looked on.

He ate a bad prawn for lunch which made his lower lip swell.

By early evening, he had the library to himself; formal hall was full, and everybody else apparently had evening plans. Igor appeared, as usual, around midnight. Toby disliked others knowing his routine, but was intrigued by his inclusion, however

137

unwittingly, in someone else's. Each night, the same two-word acknowledgment, never a word more.

The days passed—Toby spent most of them reading about the fictionalisation of the Nixon presidency, feasting on autobiographical details, drawn to the study of a professional life which ended in personal disaster, tracking the component parts of the ignominy, looking for clues, learning what he did to rise to prominence and what he did in the midst of battle, assessing what it's like to be successful and for disaster to strike, and the decision to battle on regardless—and because he was enjoying himself, and also because he didn't want to return to his rooms (they were dark and the frosted glass meant he couldn't see out; he knew the moment it was too late to change his mind he had picked badly), he stayed ever later, drawing the line at five am.

But still he was the first to leave. He started making more noise to attract Igor's attention, looking for confirmation of life and feeling awkward. He fetched books he didn't need and scraped his chair along the floor when he sat back down. He sighed and cleared his throat. He dropped folders and turned-on lamps. He relocated downstairs, hoping Igor would turn up there instead, typing up notes on a library computer and watching music videos on repeat to pass the time.

The change of scene helped Toby think. Students he didn't recognise came and went. They checked their emails, glanced at the headlines, and left after ten minutes. He listened to music, playing the same track again and again, trying to keep the feeling it gave him as the band soared through the bridge and experimented with a minor fifth in the penultimate iteration of the chorus. He fell asleep on the keyboard and awoke at seven am, sore and with eight hundred and two pages of text comprising the letters i, u, j, k, n and m.

The thing was, he was lonely, but he wasn't a loner, just someone who was yet to find his tribe. He hadn't intended for it to be this way, and nor had anyone else. He wasn't unlikeable, and friendship was more important to him than he realised. But he liked the idea of it better than its reality: he wasn't prepared to put the work in, and he disliked its transactional components. 'I'll have your back if you have mine; I'll do this for you, and you can do something for me in return.' So he resisted fulfilling his part of the bargain, and eventually the contestants faded away to transact with somebody else. He concluded friendship was a brutal business.

Toby sat down, stood up again and walked up the stairs to the mezzanine. He hadn't been up here before. It didn't form part of the introductory tour and he'd never felt sufficiently at ease to explore it of his own volition; he felt someone was always watching. It turned out there wasn't all that much to see: the ceiling was coved, and the headroom was limited; bookcases with unused, ornamental texts lined the lower part of the walls and larger ones jutted out from the balcony, segmenting the floor into sections. He checked each of them until he found the one containing Igor.

"Sorry. I was looking for T.S. Eliot."

It was the first name to come to mind. Toby didn't even like the modernists.

"He died in 1965," replied Igor.

Toby looked around. There was a sleeping bag on the floor, scrunched up against the wall Igor was using as a backrest. There were books everywhere, and scraps of paper with tiny, intense biro scribbles littered the standing room available. Igor's lips held a lit cigarette, and he was using a handheld fan to blow the smoke through an air vent. He let the ash form, dangling precariously over *Infinite Jest*, then offered the packet to Toby.

Toby declined.

"I don't smoke," he told him. "There's only so many addictions I can pretend to manage at the same time."

Igor didn't seem bothered either way.

"Do you live up here?"

"Something like that."

"I've seen worse rooms, I suppose. It lacks privacy."

Toby felt the intensity of Igor's stare, like he saw right through him, like he knew all there was to know about him and didn't find any of it particularly impressive.

"It's a long story."

"I've got time," Toby told him, surprised by his flush of confidence.

Igor crossed his legs and pushed his tongue into the side of his left cheek. There were dark bags under his eyes and his skin was the colour of heavily used bone china.

"Let's just say the college and I had a difference of opinion about the sort of activities I should be allowed to conduct in the privacy of my rooms," he said as he tapped the ash into a folded sheet of paper. "Anyway, this is better. It helps me focus."

"You seem pretty laid back about it. I would feel destroyed by something like that." Toby swallowed some saliva he didn't know what to do with.

Igor looked at him, perplexed.

"It's just a room. They're just someone's rules. They're their rules, they're not my rules. I don't want someone else's regressive ideals."

"Well, nice to meet you, anyway. They know you're here, right?"

"One assumes," said Igor, flicking through a stack of papers, his attention already on something else.

They developed a friendship. They drank and they smoked and they worked. Toby, for his part, thought it would be good while it lasted; he figured one day Igor would outgrow him, that eventually he would be done with him and cast him adrift.

Igor took him to parties, showing him the whole other world operating around him all this time, right under his nose, in the same buildings he walked past every day.

"Who's he?" Toby asked as Mark walked past them at a masked ball, sheepishly and with a little wave.

"One of my students."

"Is he any good?"

"He will be."

The next day, in the library as usual, Toby picked up the latest edition of the *TLS*. He liked to read the apologies and the clarifications and corrections. He liked the pedantry and the fussing over the smallest details. They all fundamentally agreed, as far as he could tell, so the details were all that was left. On page fourteen, he noticed Igor's by-line. He was writing about Kant and quoting somebody Swedish. He hadn't mentioned anything. Toby doubted he ever would.

"There's food in the fridge, if you're hungry," Cordelia said to him that night as he crawled into bed and into the position required so they could both sleep on the tiny little mattress. She could tell something had changed, but his body was warm, and the sheets were soft. When he touched her, there was no flutter in his heart.

*

Later that term, Toby got with a boy for the first time. It was way better than anything he'd done with a girl.

141

Mark, with his blond hair, and his beaded wrists. He had a tattoo of a small star on the hidden side of his left thigh.

"You know he's rich as?" Mark said as Toby looked around for his pants, feeling self-conscious about his body and what had taken place.

"I didn't actually." He found them behind the sofa. After the event, desire and sex just seemed so embarrassing. "How rich are we talking?"

"Pretty fucking rich." Mark resented him for it, that much was clear. "Like this living in the library thing. It's an affectation. Only someone who can afford not to gets away with it."

Mark asked him to stay.

"I can't," Toby told him, but the weeks passed, and each time, Toby swore never again.

When, eventually, he did stop, Mark called him a cheat, and self-hating.

"I'll tell her exactly what her boyfriend likes. I'll tell her exactly what sort of person he is."

"Don't be ridiculous," Toby shot back, indignant, but he told Cordelia, just in case.

When he told her he was being blackmailed, she laughed.

"It's not blackmail if he's not getting anything in return, which, by the sound of it, he no longer is." She told him to be more careful, next time. "And try not to be so naïve."

Toby struggled to accept the possibility some people had lost more of their innocence than others.

*

Igor observed all of this from afar. It was two am and he was attacking one of his cashmere hoodies with a pair of scissors.

"Ah, excellent," he said when Toby arrived. "Can you hold this bit of material, just there. Hold it tight."

Toby did as instructed. "What are we doing exactly?"

"I'm turning it into a crop top."

Igor poured out two glasses of red wine, rolled up the sleeves of his silk shirt, and tried it on for size.

"So, this girlfriend of yours." He pushed his lower lip together with his finger and thumb. "She seems pretty elusive."

"She's not at Trinity."

"I'm beginning to wonder if she exists. What did you say her name was?"

"Cordelia."

"Cordelia," Igor repeated back to himself, drawing out each syllable.

"I like to keep stuff separate."

"It's pretty weird we've never met her, though."

"She's got her own stuff going on."

"If you say so."

"Do you have any pics?"

"Not on me, no."

"Have you met her family?"

"Some of them. They're impressive. They're…achievers."

Igor took a slug of his wine.

"You know," he said to Toby, "when you talk about people you're close to, you tend to focus on their achievements, or their famous family, or their potential for success. You never say, 'He's my friend because I like being in his life and I like him being in mine.'"

In time, Toby came to realise Igor had skewered him in a sentence.

*

Term was ending, the spell around college was wearing off, and people were planning their next move. Meanwhile, Toby was in full-scale retreat. He would be kicked out of halls to make room for the conference crowd; there was Cordelia's place of course, but staying there felt to him like a cop-out, an admission of dependence. He had no appetite to return home, another admission, but knew he probably would. In the bedroom where he'd grown up, the furniture exactly as it was when he last lived there, all of it was the same, but it seemed smaller now, and further away from him. He remembered the dream.

He tried raising it with Igor, but Igor was steadfast in his refusal to talk about family. He never talked about his family, ever, and so Toby knew nothing of Igor's boarding school upbringing, or his mother's hard-nosed portrayal of the absent father he had never known.

"Why do you need to go home at all?" Igor asked him one evening on the mezzanine.

"I'm—expected."

"Are you now?" He looked around for the corkscrew. "Has anyone told you that, specifically?"

"It's implied."

He thought of his life as a well-shaped story, he as its conscious author, focused on its curation. The shape of the thing would be prioritised above all else.

"I see."

"What will you do?" Toby asked.

"I'll be here." He spread his arms wide. "King of the Castle."

"Sounds depressing."

"Nope. I think you'd like it. You get the place to yourself."

Toby wondered if Igor used the time to catch-up, but it seemed unlikely. He never seemed behind.

"You know your problem?" Igor asked him, perching forward on the front of his feet, intent on telling him. "You lack courage of conviction. You retreat at the first sign of resistance."

Igor took a drag on his Lucky Strike, then crushed the butt beneath his heel.

"I'm not telling you this to be a dick. I just think it's a brittle form of salvation if you're always waiting for permission."

"Well, not everyone has that luxury."

Igor sipped at his wine.

"Even so, there's no point living big decisions only in your mind."

*

It was the commemoration ball. It was white tie, it was full-length evening dresses, it was class warfare at the hot food stand.

"Just grab as many as you can," a tall woman in a satin grey dress yelled to her friend at the front of the queue, referring to the hot dogs.

Someone told her off for bad behaviour.

"Excuse me, madam," she replied, indignant. It was the 'madam' which gave her away, and Toby's heart broke for her.

He collected two glasses of champagne, lukewarm but bubbly at least, and passed one of them to Cordelia.

"Igor said he'd be over shortly," he told her.

For Toby, the whole point of attending was for the two of them to meet, but it was Igor and three hundred of his closest friends, and Toby was beginning to realise he hadn't properly thought it through. He adopted an outlandish persona to conceal his unease. The music helped, as did the cabaret, and the burlesque, but he didn't really like what they'd done to the college; it lacked restraint and looked superimposed.

Toby and Cordelia queued for the dodgems and, to pass the time, watched tipsy undergrads go wild on the carousel. The night had barely started, but he had a low tolerance for crowds.

When Igor jumped the queue and made a fuss over Cordelia, speaking at length about his gladness she did, in fact, exist, Toby could see he was already fucked, but still, he looked impeccable in his single-breasted tailcoat and black dress trousers, two lines of braid running down the outside leg.

Cordelia immediately liked him, that much was obvious, but Toby wasn't sure Igor liked her. Toby wasn't sure *he* even liked her that much in the dress she had chosen. It emphasised all the bits she should have tried to conceal: skeletal, hillocky little breasts, narrow hips evoking the barest minimum of womanliness, dainty shoulders which reminded him of porcelain.

Toby liked dodgems, always had, and in these days before he had discovered the depth of pleasure only alcohol could give him, he favoured party games over endless small talk and low-level flirting. Mark smashed into him with as much force as he could, the contours of his face altered by the four gin gimlets he'd downed in his Garden Quad room, pre-loading.

They regrouped in the marquee waiting for the band to begin their set, hovering on the outskirts of the mosh pit. Igor made an innuendo which Cordelia didn't pick up, but he recovered quickly, and moved seamlessly into the version of the conversation Cordelia thought they was having. It was striking to watch. It was selfless, and kind, and good conversation technique, it was all those things, but most of all it demonstrated his capacity to control.

When Mark sought them out, Igor complimented him on his driving prowess.

"I can't lie," Mark replied. "I am good on a dodgem. What about you, Toby?"

"I like to think I can hold my own." These were the first words they had exchanged in weeks.

"Well, you certainly kept it a secret. People have so many secrets. It's so interesting, don't you think?"

"I love a secret," said Igor.

"Toby, what do you think?" Mark asked.

"What was the question?"

"You heard me. Secrets, they're so interesting."

"I guess," Toby replied. "Or perhaps there are some things most people are just too polite to talk about."

When the band started to play, Igor took Mark to one side.

"I just want an explanation," said Mark, still brazen and unapologetic.

"Why do people always look for explanations?" replied Igor. "Sometimes there is no explanation. People are strange, that's the explanation."

Cordelia professed not to like the music, and suggested Toby take her on a tour of the college instead. She hadn't spent any time in Trinity; Toby had never invited her in before, and she knew how angry he would be if she turned up unannounced.

But it wasn't the best time for it; whole sections were blocked off, and the light was fading. They tried one of the back routes, through the narrow strip of woodland. There was a strong smell of weed and lots of giggling, and they had to navigate their way around the legs sticking out of the bushes, only to discover the path leading to Library Quad was closed.

Toby apologised, although he wasn't all that disappointed. He didn't want her to be part of it; he didn't even want her to see it. But as they made their way back to the thoroughfare, he couldn't resist asking if she liked Igor.

"You obviously do," she replied.

"I don't like him like that."

"I didn't say you did."

"He's—interesting, is all."

"I can see that."

"Is he what you expected?"

"Toby, he is exactly what I expected."

Sometimes she wondered if he even realised the loyalty she had given him. Did he place any value at all on her sacrifice?

They lined up for drinks at the cash-only bar, housed in a repurposed metal-tubed camper van. The queue moved slowly; someone at the front was insisting on sampling two different white wines before placing his order.

"Can you believe this guy?" Freddie asked them as he turned around.

He didn't know Toby was behind him—he would have spoken to anyone, genetically good-natured—but he remembered Toby's name, and he remembered he had never met Cordelia.

Toby introduced them.

"This is Freddie. He's been teaching me about rowing."

Freddie had recently found Toby puzzling at the results chalked onto a college wall, trying to decipher the code: who was winning, and according to whose rules?

"Oh, really," Cordelia replied.

Freddie asked about their summer plans.

"Me?" said Toby. "I haven't thought about it." When he did, all he felt was relief.

"'Haven't really thought about it,'" Freddie repeated back to him. "I get it. Exams. No extra band width currently available."

Cordelia asked what he would be doing.

"Bit of travel, we're thinking," he said, without clarifying who he meant by 'we'. "South America. Hostels and hiking."

"Nice," replied Toby.

"You done much travelling?" Freddie asked.

"Not really."

At times, England felt like the other side of the world, or at least this bit of England did, sometimes. He was intimidated by their money, and their confidence, the way they made him feel otherised; a Scot abroad, in it, but not of it.

Toby and Cordelia abandoned the occasion long before the seven am survivors' photo but, before they left, Igor found a way to take Cordelia aside to tell her she and Toby had to let each other go.

"You're holding each other back. It can't work, long-term. It's a dishonest way to live."

"Love knows many expressions, Igor," Cordelia replied, perhaps excessively assertive.

Igor spent the rest of the early hours flirting with one of the waiters, but by the time his shift ended, Igor had lost interest and was fucking someone else in the disabled toilets, using the liquid soap as lube.

| **PART SIX** |
WHAT GETS REWARDED,
GETS REPEATED

2020

We hope the best of who and what we are will subsist, but nothing is forever; eventually, even the most sacred of our days are cast aside.

Freddie was sad about it, the hurt his decision would cause, and the scars his children would bear.

*

Meanwhile in East Dulwich, Cordelia was shopping for twigs.

"This one will sprout little green leaves if you treat it well," the florist told her. They were staring at a stick of gnarled bark which looked like a pitchfork.

"I'll take two."

She had arranged to meet her mother at ten o'clock, but ten o'clock became eleven o'clock and, at ten to eleven, eleven o'clock became noon, and when the conveniently located bakery became 'why don't you just come round to the house,' Cordelia was starting to feel she was doing all the running.

Today, she had been up at three, up again at four and Freddie woke her at five when he tripped on his way out of the shower.

She pushed the twins towards the car, ignoring the homeless man on the pavement who, provocatively placed, asked her for change as she assembled her family and strapped them in. As she tossed the twigs into the boot, she stared at him her fullest look of contempt.

She rang the doorbell. It started well enough, with the twigs and the air kisses and the glow of what was once familiar.

"Do they need food and water?" Mrs. Green asked, Cordelia presumed, of the twigs.

Many years had passed since Cordelia last lived in this house, but her mother's clout over her, and her capacity to diminish her, remained ever powerful still.

"Where's dad?" Cordelia asked.

"He's around."

As Mrs. Green joined the children on the floor, she was contemplative. How enviably small was their knowledge of the world. How little they knew of its ways, and the demands it would make of them. Was that why she only ever spoke to them as she would to an adult?

The children served as a useful buffer between mother and daughter, and the altered dynamic softened their competing perspectives: now she was a mother, Cordelia seemed, to Mrs. Green, an older figure, more mature, less prone to the dramatic; and now she was a grandmother, Mrs. Green seemed, to Cordelia, younger, less hectoring, less preachy.

"Have you seen your friend Igor, recently?"

"We're allowed to talk about him now, are we?"

Cordelia didn't see much of Igor at all, these days. Their lives were so different, by choice but also—and this, surely, the tragedy of it, Cordelia concluded as she passed the twins an age-inappropriate toy—by happenstance. Igor told her once he had too strong a sense of self to subordinate it to a vocation or a job or a marriage, and his revelation made him less interesting to her. They were suffering a deficit of universality.

"Perhaps it is for the best," Mrs. Green observed, lightly. Not that she need worry. Cordelia had sworn her secrecy. She was a conspirator.

Catching herself, Mrs. Green put any remaining thoughts on the issue to the back of her mind, and turned her attention elsewhere. "Why would your mother dress you in this?" she said as she folded back the fabric, looking for a label. She had a very specific view of what constituted good value. "I mean, really Cordelia. I can only imagine the cost of this. Feel the fabric. So thin! You could have made this."

*

"All these boys whom you fuck," Tristan noted. "Isn't it boring after a while, the endless parade of flesh?"

"I'm interested in anatomical variation." Igor was lying. He was growing immune to the excitement he once felt; increasingly, he didn't even want to touch them, all he required was to see them denuded, so he could assess whether he had imagined correctly.

"Boys aren't like iPhones, you know," said Tristan. "You can't just smash the back in and demand an upgrade." He laughed at his own joke. "Do any of them even know what they're doing?"

"Some are a bit green, sure, but they manage."

Tristan drank his drink, indifferent to it. "Are any of them even close to boyfriend material?"

Igor affected indifference.

"As in, actually capable of caring for you, or you, really, for them."

Igor repositioned himself on the sofa.

"How's Dominick?" Igor asked.

"He's fine."

"You're still *servicing* him?"

"I might be."

That evening, Igor poured himself a double measure of Grey Goose, which in homage to Toby he had taken to drinking neat, then answered the knock at the door. He was doing this more frequently; haggling for hook-ups, well, the appeal of that had started to wane—these days, he preferred the neatness of a formal transaction, and money made him less inhibited about doing exactly what he wanted with and to them. This one had a nice accent, although Igor didn't give him the chance to say much. Igor liked his narrow hips, his bony shoulders and his big lanky feet; he was young and keen and pulsating an ill-at-ease energy. They were done in twenty-five minutes.

"Stay for a drink, if you want," he said afterwards, despite himself. He'd paid for the hour.

Igor sensed his reticence. "What," he asked him. "Will your boyfriend get jealous?"

"I don't do boyfriends. I think guys are disgusting."

It was hard to tell if he meant it. His porcelain pout made him hard to read to the point of inscrutable. It never left him, even in bed, not even when he came.

"I guess I'll take a vodka tonic."

Igor mixed the drinks as the boy cast around a judgemental eye. Tristan's latest video was displayed on Igor's iMac, paused at a flattering moment. The boy pressed the space bar and Tristan twitched into life.

"That was my idea, you know," Igor told him, sipping from a glass which contained more vodka than mixer. It tasted reassuringly like paint stripper.

"YouTube?"

"That's right. YouTube was my idea. That's what I'm telling you."

An eye-roll, then: "I'm a subscriber, actually. I like him."

"You and two million others," Igor replied.

Tristan's channel had definitely become a thing. It was actually happening, and he was at the centre of it. Tristan realised so much of it was a trick of the mind; once you believed you could, so did everyone else. He was the one, he told himself, who had created something from nothing, and he had done it with no safety net, no one to call on, no one to bail him out of the abyss.

He was reviewing the latest batch of works offers, assessing which would provide the most exposure for the least effort, then picked up his phone to monitor the reaction to his latest video, part of a mini-series; over 40,000 likes, lower than he expected at this point in the cycle. He scrolled through the comments from viewers not subscribed to his channel and placed emojis on the ones he liked.

"Tristan," Dominick snapped, "are you listening to me?"

"Not really, no."

It was a Thursday morning in late October, very early, just as the sky was brightening. They lay side by side as the room grew warm.

Tristan turned to face him, to look at him, at his beauty, at everything he was in this moment.

"I'm out tonight," said Dominick. "I'm seeing *him*."

"I wish you wouldn't." How Tristan wished he could barricade off all that came before what they now had.

Toby's father, the self-defined "colossus" (*"What is 8% of a quarter? It's fuck-all, that's what it is!"*)—Dominick still saw him regularly, assembled in the private dining room of the patriarch, just the two of them, surrounded by portraits of distinguished men and stuffy, old-school art, matching him glass for glass (quickly and greedily, three gulps per flute).

Tristan thought of it as Dominick's search for redemption, that somewhere, and with a depth of feeling which was irreversible, he blamed himself, that it was his fault.

The issue of Toby. Tristan rather hoped Dominick would no longer want to talk about it, that he would be bored thinking about it, bored of carrying it around. He resented Toby's enduring influence; he wanted it off the agenda, even if that meant each of them playing along, pretending to have forgotten. It was a conundrum: Dominick's experience, his wrestling with loss, it had devastated him, but also it was the making of him, and the flailing around in the dark brought them together, guiding each other to a salvation. But must they endure Toby's shadow forever more? Tristan liked to believe Dominick wouldn't go back, even if he could. He liked to believe he and Toby would be totally unrecognisable to each other. He wanted to believe Dominick would always have chosen him.

*

When Igor took the call, it felt like he'd been summoned, and the lady on the line was oddly coy.

"Am I speaking to E-gor?" Mrs. Green asked.

"It's I-gor." He summoned his phone voice, pushed the steeliest version of himself to the fore.

"I-gor," she repeated back to him, slow and unsure.

She had seen his advert: *He painted each wall of my house a different colour and I couldn't be happier. It's like living in a rubric's cube!" "He painted me out of my divorce!" "My staff loved the way he applied the eggshell, our best sales figures yet!"*

He arrived that afternoon to a house which wasn't nearly as grand as the voice at the end of the line. It was lavish, and from certain angles it might even pass for opulent, but it was the house of someone who'd had to work for it.

Mrs. Green opened the door, slow and deliberate, and Igor observed her noble, patrician look, the creases of her neck disguised by a pearl necklace, and her body flattened by heavy cashmere. Her hair was grey, but she wore it in a bob, evoking her fashionista prowess of younger days.

"Come in," she instructed, looking at Igor intensely. "You'll take off your shoes?"

She stood before him as he did so, radiating a condescending benevolence, then walked him round the house. "Paint everything," she instructed him. She wanted him there for as long as possible. She wanted to see him up close.

"My husband can be a difficult man," she told him, "in case you see him when you are here."

A dog barked outside, and she jumped.

"We used to have a hound," she told Igor, clutching his right arm. "She was a terrible flirt, always getting herself into trouble."

Igor set to work, firmly of the view nothing was beyond repair, determined to save all he could; it required of him an exactitude he rarely bothered to apply—painting was a side-gig, he did it for his own amusement—but, this time, aware of all that was at stake, he proceeded carefully, cautious to the point of fastidious; there was something overtly destructive about the intent of Mrs. Green's instructions.

Mrs. Green looked on throughout, a ringside seat, apparently, at the greatest show on earth. Her attention put him off his stride, and when she realised this, eventually, she busied herself with superfluous tasks: unpacking boxes only to pack them again, rehanging frames on unfinished walls, washing his

159

paintbrushes the moment he set them down. She took her time explaining the simplest of subject matters. In the bathroom, as he surveyed nudes and messaged the prettiest, he had a feeling she was outside, devising a reason to join him, or looking for a way to break down the door.

"You know my daughter, I think. Cordelia." None of this was lost on him. He knew the game she played.

"And her husband."

"From university, I gather."

Rarely did Igor think of that time. He wanted to tell Mrs. Green her daughter cut him off as soon as motherhood beckoned, that literally he had not heard from her since the twins were born, but there was a cruelty in the statement of that sort of criticism, and, in truth, he had noticed their commonality disperse over a longer number of years, Cordelia one of many, as each of his friends moved off in different directions; the exodus to Hong Kong and to New York City and to Singapore and to Sydney the first signs of trouble, and from there the slow slipping away into the shadows. He didn't begrudge them wanting change in their lives, but must it always be at his expense?

Mrs. Green asked of his parents.

"My mother is a businesswoman."

"And your father?"

"Missing in action."

"You've never known him?"

"Never did, never want to."

"How terrible," she said, sincerely. "You are still his son; what he is, you are too."

*

160

"So, you've met the Greens, then?" asked Freddie of Igor.

"Only the wife."

Mr. Green remained absent still. He didn't use the bathroom, he didn't eat, he didn't drink. He stayed elsewhere, upstairs, downstairs, silent, seemingly not moving at all.

"Count yourself lucky. The old man is a bastard."

"I got that impression." Igor, noticing the circles under Freddie's eyes, and his hair, cut shorter than it should have been, making him look like an elf, pointed towards the window leading onto the roof. "Shall we?"

"You know I don't smoke," said Freddie, with a grin, as he reached into his pocket for a carefully concealed, wafer-thin cigarettes' holder.

He and Igor positioned themselves on the slate tiles atop the roof of the Greens' household and looked around. The sky was blue, and the sun was shining onto the November frost, and Freddie said matter of factly he was using websites to meet women for sex. He was not constitutionally ruminative, and so his forthright admission made structural sense, at least to him, but saying it at all made Igor jumpy.

"Is it just sex?" he asked.

"I'm not having an affair, if that's what you mean. I would never do that."

"So moral."

He had far more than most, according at least to all the usual barometers, but he would never have as much as Igor, and perhaps that was why he was uncharacteristically loose-tongued: he didn't think of himself as ungrateful, yet still he lusted for the sensual pleasures of the libertine's world.

They heard raised voices downstairs, then tears.

"Fuck my life," Freddie said under his breath. He associated his children with tedium, with shackled responsibility, with the

161

seven to eleven working day. It was harder than he thought it should be.

"Too late now," Igor told him, instinctively playing his part. "*Till death do we part!* No one made you say it."

Freddie snorted. "I meant it at the time. No one said I had to mean it forever."

Igor exhaled a cloud of smoke as he looked onto the skeletal trees: the branches were bare, clinging on for spring.

"What do you think I should do?" Freddie asked him.

"I wish you hadn't told me at all."

"I didn't plan to," Freddie replied, flicking away some ash.

Igor took a heavy drag on his Lucky Strike. "Do what you want." Igor could foresee the divorce proceedings, the judge awarding the children and most of Freddie's money to their mother. "You're fucked either way."

Freddie, though—a testament to his character, and all he was brought up to be—appeared unperturbed. "I wonder how she would respond."

"Cordelia?"

"She's practical. Maybe all she'd want is the washing machine."

"I wouldn't count on it."

They finished their cigarettes.

"I'm horrible to her, but still, she clings on, and it makes me hate her more."

"Hate?"

Freddie let the word hang. There was something claustrophobic about her love, and her lust for busyness at all costs disguised a growing inability, he sensed, to be at one with herself. He wanted her to hate him a little.

"It never used to be this hard," said Freddie, as Igor and he made their way back to the window. "It's getting harder to avoid

162

the bad stuff." Freddie shivered; it was as cold in here as it was out there. "This is the truth no one wants to tell you, because if you knew, you would do all you could never to grow up."

He searched his pockets, suddenly panicked. "Fuck. I don't have any mints."

The house took another three weeks to finish. Everything took longer than it should, Igor's perfectionism a noose round his neck, and the mistakes correlated to his frustrations. Yet he would, in time, come to feel gratitude for his pedantry. Without it, he might never have found the photos.

He wasn't snooping—other people's secrets rarely interested him—and the photo stash which tumbled out of the right-hand pillar of desk drawers when he lost his grip of them would barely have merited mention, but for the startling discovery all the photography was of him. The photographs, he could tell at a glance, went back years, a diverse portfolio of the chapters of his life, and something about their clumsy curation—haphazardly thrown together, unfiled, and curiously unlabelled in a house where even the herbs were catalogued—implied that, for these people, in this place, he was as much a source of shame as he was a source of interest.

Igor heard footsteps approaching the door.

"Are you injured?" Mrs. Green asked.

She tried to assess what had fallen and what he might have found. Igor's doctoral thesis was located on the shelf immediately next to him. How could he not have seen it?

"No," he answered her. "Neither is the desk."

Igor looked at Mrs. Green. What did she know? What did she know that he did not?

Three days later, Cordelia sat down with her phone and scrolled through her messages. Most were from customer services; she complained a lot, took great pleasure in writing scathing reviews online.

"Are you getting anything from this, though?" Freddie asked her often. "Because they don't care, that's for sure."

It was displacement activity, she knew, this raging against the machine, an outlet for all she wanted to say to her mother but could not.

Her mother's brutal methodology was, to Cordelia, contemptable, but she did admire its efficiency: the handling was unpleasant, no question, and she knew, on some level, it was delusional, devising a fiction and expecting all her collaborators to hold the line, but still—what a thing to behold.

Bluntly, she had grown not to care: Igor was not her brother; she did not want that complication, and already he was as much a part of her life as he ever would be.

She knew the selfishness of it: Igor, not knowing which of his traits came from which of his parents, Igor's view of his father as a feckless betrayer uncorrected, and no doubt consolidated as his knowledge of the capacity of man grew.

But, Cordelia understood, and with her mother's position she agreed.

On her phone, there were five or so messages from Igor, all of them asking for attention in as low key a way as possible, although, in the most recent message, he had given up the disguise and simply asked her to call him. She pressed at his name on the screen and heard the dial tone.

"It's one in the morning," Igor complained, answering on the second ring. "You can't call people at this time."

She asked him what he wanted to talk about, but of course already she knew, and she listened to him at the end of the line working through the possibilities, terrified of what he might say next. She was playing for time, making sure she got the story straight. Her mother had been very specific about what she could and could not say.

"It doesn't make any sense," Igor told her, aware each of them held a secret from the other. He monitored her breath as he said it but couldn't detect anything of note. Maybe she was similarly accomplished when it came to lying. Or maybe she knew nothing at all. He offered specificity: "our photos with Toby, when you were letting him do you,"—(the absurdity of it still amused him)—"that actress year of yours,"—referring, really, to Seb in the Pleasance, backstage passes hanging round his neck, looking prepossessing and mischievous, but also, of course, to Camilla (and to that, Cordelia remarked: *"God, I loved her! So wonderful!"*)—and there was YouTube, also, a still of a video he recorded with Tristan. It occurred to him how little any of these images said anything about him of note.

"The photos are mine, Igor," said Cordelia. "I'm sentimental like that. I like hard copies of the good times."

It saddened them both she talked in the past tense, like the best days were behind them, that there was less living left to be done.

"It just doesn't make a lot of sense."

"Most things usually don't."

He feigned indifference. "How's Freddie?" he asked, and the casualness of her answer confirmed she knew nothing of her husband's plans. At the beginning of the call, Igor thought he might remedy that oversight, but not now.

| PART SEVEN |
LOVE HAS NO MORTAL END

2021

The giving of love outright—blind with love, and blind to all its folly; only the fool gives all his heart.

*

As Tristan scanned the room, disconcerted by all these people from his life assembled under one roof, he overheard the photographer ask a guest to stop 'ifucking the camera'.

"I was not," the guest replied, his tone indignant.

"You were, though."

"No, really," the guest insisted, reddening as he turned to his friend. "I mean, I don't even like having my photo taken."

*

Cordelia stood nervously; her shoulders shrivelled up into her body.

"Have you seen him?" she asked Dominick. "Recently, I mean."

He had been touring the grounds, one final inspection.

Without Freddie, her social currency had fallen in value, but she didn't make it easy for herself, either. She was so openly vulnerable, and it made her difficult company. She didn't care, seemingly; it was her pain, and she was in hell, and she would not sugar coat it for them.

"No, not recently," Dominick replied.

She had promised herself she wouldn't forage for information, but now she was here, and everyone seemed so unaffected, it was hard to resist.

"Is he coming?"

Dominick lied and said he didn't know.

"But he was invited?"

"I think so."

She looked away, hurt but not surprised. The children clung to her legs, bored. A couple at the other end of the room waved to her and she acknowledged them briefly.

"The way other mothers look at me," she said to Dominick. She closed her eyes and shuddered. "I can't bear their pity."

Maybe it isn't pity, Dominick suggested. "Maybe they sympathise. Maybe they fear it happening to them. None of us is immune."

"Some of them blame me, you can hear it in their tone. That I drove him away, or I missed the warning signs. I mean, who teaches you the clues? They should put *that* on the syllabus."

Dominick was concerned she was talking so openly in front of the children.

"Sorry, I'm not myself." She swallowed the remains of her gin martini. "It's just—and let this be a lesson to you," she added, prodding him in the chest lightly, "you think you've built something solid, and it turns out all it takes to destroy is for one of you to walk out the front door and never look back."

She clutched Dominick's arm, suddenly manic.

"I didn't even want this life. He had to persuade me! And now I'm stuck and he's—free! How fucked up is that." She took a breath. "There must be someone else. No one just leaves. And you know what that means, don't you?"

Dominick said he didn't.

"It means my children will be brought up by another woman. 'I'm going to call you step-mum,' they'll say, 'because if you're important to dad, you're important to us.'"

Her eyes looked wild.

"And this one," she said, pointing at her daughter, "this one tells me she secretly prefers spending time with daddy, even though he's never here. I mean, what do you even say to that?"

Dominick feared children; the only truly serious questions are the ones even a child can formulate.

"I'm sure he's not proud of his behaviour, Cordelia."

"He's not proud of it, but he did it anyway."

A waiter approached with canapés and the children took two each.

"I don't even know why," said Cordelia, her stomach in knots. "He won't even tell me why."

*

"Shall we even do this?" Dominick asked Tristan in the bridal suite bathroom.

Tristan turned off the tap, unconcerned.

"Don't be leaving me at the altar, please," he replied, focusing on his recently threaded eyebrows.

"Of course not." Dominick tugged the knot of his tie loose, reconciled to another attempt. "We'd just have the master of ceremonies announce an indefinite postponement."

"Can you imagine?" Tristan laughed, feigning horror. "'*The ceremony is postponed due to unforeseen circumstances.*'"

He moved into their lounge, looking for his sporran.

"Anyway, this is no time to go wobbly on me," he shouted behind him. "We've already paid."

*

Downstairs, Igor worked the room. He always had something good to say about people and, when he spoke, he was case specific. He was regaling a group of middle-aged women with a colourful account of Tristan and Dominick's first date when his mother approached, knocking him off his stride.

"Mother," he said, a touch of irony in his voice. They hadn't seen each other in eighteen months and, even then, it had been at his instigation.

"Son," she replied, matching his tone.

He introduced her to the group. She was on her third glass of champagne, and it was smoothing down some of her harder edges, yet even chemically altered, all she could muster was a tight little smile which told them to keep their distance, struggling, as ever, with the intimacy of others.

He took her to one side before she started talking about her money.

"What is it?" she asked him.

"Nothing."

He didn't like her ability to read him, despite all the years she had chosen to spend without him.

"Spit it out."

"Really."

"Right this second, Igor. I cannot bear it when people don't speak their mind."

"I wanted to talk about my father."

There, he told himself, he'd said it.

She took a sip of her champagne. "You see. This is exactly what I mean. You *are* bourgeois these days." She waved at someone in the distance. "From where is all this coming?" she asked him, defiantly grammatical. "I thought we were done with this."

She looked at him, searching his expression for an answer.

"Oh, I see. Yes, I see it now. It's all this wedding shit. Well, don't worry. It will pass."

Igor looked at her, weary of her stubbornness.

"Let me say this, though. And I say this speaking as your mother. It's better never to have known, than to find out the full horror of the truth."

"You know," he told her, suddenly exasperated, "up close, you're starting to look really old."

She was unfazed.

"And remember," she continued, "he never wanted you in his life. You don't want to look desperate."

It was problematic for Igor, the ease with which Mr. Green had created a life in which he didn't exist, that part of his history rewritten.

She scooped up a fourth glass from a passing tray and winked at the teenaged waiter, touching Igor's arm as he drew her further into the corner.

"Exactly how green do you think I am, mother?"

"Do *not* even speak that man's name. Really, Igor, I am imploring you. Leave this alone. If not for me, do it for you. You don't need someone like that. Why should you welcome him into your life when he did—everything—in his power to exclude you from his? He would have aborted you, if you must know. He gave me the money for it."

"What did you spend it on instead?" Igor asked.

"My first business."

Freddie's date struggled with her heels as they marched determinedly over the cobbles and towards the entrance.

"Are you planning on telling me anything about these people?" she asked him. She was wearing a canary yellow dress which did nothing for her complexion.

Freddie didn't immediately answer her.

"Who, specifically?"

"Maybe start with the grooms?"

"They're just some guys." He was distracted, assessing who was where. "I've known them forever. You'll like them."

"Are they friends with your ex-wife?"

He had told her they were divorced (they weren't), that it was a starter marriage (only in retrospect), that it was no big deal (thought no one).

"I assume so," he replied.

Freddie walked in first. Immediately in front of him was Mr. Green, who stared at him, looked right through him, then summoned the necessary body language to convey that in no circumstances should he seek to engage him in conversation. Freddie had changed his mind about the Greens now they were open about their contempt for him. He admired them that.

Freddie took two flutes of champagne from a serving tray and scanned the rooms for someone safe to approach. He avoided his reflection in the mirror above the ornately etched fireplace and guided his date in the direction of the ceiling-high pillars, a gravitational pull towards a solid structure he could use to hide.

"We can sit over there," he said, pointing to the stained-glass window and the bench built into the panelling beneath it, "if you want to sit down."

She shook her head and took one of the flutes from him.

A quartet played Schumann in the far corner of the room.

"Do you know any of the family?" she asked.

Freddie delayed his answer and was relieved when he saw Igor approach.

"You're not even Scottish," Freddie told him, referring to his kilt.

"Today, I am," explained Igor as his tartan of greys and greens billowed around him.

From the safety of the other side of the library, Cordelia observed the three of them huddled together. Freddie looked well, she thought, tanned and less bulky than on the day he left; she could see no distress in the contours of his face, there was no wound. The girl standing next to him was pretty, she would give him that, albeit in a mainstream sort of way. But the generosity of her smile, Cordelia concluded, made her look desperate. She shouldn't be here at all! It was needlessly cruel.

At least she'd brought the children, she told herself, although she knew—on some level—they would hate her for it eventually, when they were old enough to realise she too was playing a game.

Igor, his eyes everywhere, noticed her looking.

"You're sitting next to my mother by the way," he said to Freddie.

Freddie sighed. "God. That really is terrible."

"The worst," Igor added.

"Why?"

"Someone has to."

"But why me?"

"You know why."

"No one deserves that. Really."

Cordelia was offended by Freddie's brazenness, by his enduring capacity for joy.

She propelled herself towards him, in control but also not, the children following in pursuit. She felt her despondence mutate into fire.

Igor saw her on the periphery of his vision and turned to greet her, reaching to touch her shoulder in solidarity. She flinched, mistaking it for pity.

"This gin is really very good," she said, letting the empty martini glass hang loosely in her hand.

"It's the best," Igor agreed. "I'll get more."

He summoned his favourite of the waiters and tried to talk to Cordelia through the children, a coded appeal to reason.

When Cordelia stuck out her hand in the direction of Freddie's date, she kept her elbow by her side.

"I'm Freddie's wife."

Her martini arrived.

It was three months since the children had last seen their father. In theory, he was Saturdays only, an arrangement with which he was perfectly content, but committing to all the Saturdays, month in, month out, was proving logistically difficult. The children were important, but they were not the only demands on his time.

Cordelia lifted the martini glass from the tray and slid one of the olives along the cocktail stick with her front teeth and into her mouth. She chewed it and poked her tongue around her veneers to clear the fragments from her gums.

The randomness of what she once thought of as her decisions! She had fallen in love with Freddie, but had it not been he, it would have been someone else, and, in that man, she would have invested the same hopes and dreams. But for Toby, they might never have met. How she wished they never had; the man whom she once thought the greatest of the gifts bestowed on her, in fact the opposite.

Freddie kneeled and reached out his arms to the children.

"Don't come any closer," Cordelia told him, blocking his path. "Can't you see they're scared of you?"

They didn't look scared. They were nervous, perhaps, but that was her doing, and he was confident he could re-establish the old camaraderie. It hadn't occurred to him she would use the children as leverage. She was always so clear she couldn't abide parents who did that.

"I mean it," she said. "You no longer have the right."

"Don't, Cordelia. Please."

The words slipped out of him.

"'Don't, please,'" she sneered. "Maybe that's what I should have said. 'Don't go. Don't, please.'"

She tossed her martini at him.

Freddie flinched when he saw the glass jerk forward in his direction and he felt his anger rise as the liquid ran down onto and then through his shirt.

"Don't just stand there," Cordelia said to him.

She looked at Igor.

"He's doing it deliberately. He thinks if he does nothing, it's all on me. Well," she said, turning to face Freddie once more, "you will not shame me into submission. I refuse, and I will tell everyone exactly what it is you have done. I will tell them exactly what you are."

She spoke quietly, but her tone was close to fever pitch. She looked at the children—they were riveted—and at the plus one, who was stony-faced. She didn't know, Cordelia realised, suddenly.

"I'm sorry you're angry," said Freddie.

"Anger does not begin to describe what I feel towards you."

177

Perhaps it was his self-control, or his defiant, martyred look, or perhaps it was his implication he didn't recognise the version of himself Cordelia now threatened to expose.

Perhaps it was because he didn't even seem sorry.

She struck him with all her weight. She used her forearms.

He did not even raise his arms as a shield.

Igor pulled her back and suggested she stop, which she did.

People were looking, that was Mrs. Green's first thought as she rushed forward and told Freddie to go.

"Go, right now," she told him, pointing at the exit.

"It is not for you to demand my departure," Freddie replied.

For the first time, Cordelia saw in him all the contempt he had come to feel for her. "You've humiliated me," she shouted at him, "and you continue to humiliate me. What did I ever do to you to deserve this? Do you even know the ghastliness of what you have unleashed into our lives?" She took a step back, brought her right hand to her temples. "Just, get away from me. If you have any sense of shame, get away from me."

Outside, Freddie felt immediately better, though Cordelia's selfishness lingered in his mind. He was tired of continually mitigating for it; she did not see the loss he had suffered at the hands of—this *mutual* event, intent, as she was, on attributing to him sole blame. Witnessing her fizzing and frothing like that, championing her need for exceptionalism, it reconfirmed all he wished to escape. They were a family like any other family, they were together and now they were not, but they would remain together still, in a hybrid, and he would continue to give them his money and he would continue to offer his support. It was what it was.

"To be honest," he told his date as they reconvened on the cobbles—they had been inside the venue for less than forty minutes—"you can probably go now. I'll still pay you the full amount, but I think you should go. It will look better this way. But thank you for coming. It just makes it easier if she has cause to paint me as the villain."

It didn't matter to her either way, so she ordered an Uber, reminded him he hadn't said goodbye to his children, and turned towards the car park to wait for the driver.

*

"I am mortified, Cordelia. Mortified." It was the lapse in etiquette which offended Mrs. Green most; she had no time for hysteria. "What were you thinking?"

"So now it's my fault, is it?"

"Really," Mrs. Green carried on. "And in front of the children."

"Oh, the children know. *They know.*"

"Of course they know, but is that how you want them to see you behave?"

Mrs. Green took off her hat.

"Let me look at you." She inspected Cordelia's dress. The lace detailing had survived unscathed, she discovered to her relief, but one of the buttons on the back was loose. She reached into her bag for her sewing kit.

"Hold still," she instructed, setting to work in the expectation the quietude of the task would reimpose decorum.

"All I'm saying is, don't make the children take sides when it's clear they are already on yours."

Mrs. Green slid the thread through the eye of the needle, then doubled it over and knotted the ends.

"But they deserve to know who their father is," said Cordelia. "I want them—I want everyone—to know exactly who he is."

"It's not that he's this or he's that, though, really, is it."

Mrs. Green ran the needle through to the front of the material, then back again.

"It's just how he is. I don't profess to understand it. It's a strange choice, but it's his to make."

She centred the button and stitched it back into position, using a pin as a spacer.

"I don't deny he's selfish," she added, looping the remaining material around the threads beneath the button. She pulled on it tightly and tied it off, making a small knot on the underside of the fabric.

"There," she exclaimed. "Good as new."

Cordelia turned round; the colour still drained from her face.

"I can't bear it," she said, her legs ready to buckle.

"Do not give him the satisfaction. Not even for a second," Mrs. Green commanded of her. "You thought he was better than this, but it turns out he's not. Now you know. Maybe you always knew. Maybe you knew and chose not to look. It's not for me to say," she said, saying it. "Or maybe it was just convenient for him to stay, until it was more convenient for him to leave."

Mrs. Green assessed how to conceal the despair etched onto her daughter's face.

"You will be fine. The children will be fine. I don't want to hear any more negative talk." Mrs. Green reached into her bag, searching for make-up to repair Cordelia's mascara. "Talk like that takes you nowhere. Making a spectacle of yourself takes you nowhere."

Mrs. Green told Cordelia to hold still as she moved the mascara wand towards her daughter's eyelashes. She shook her head. "Your generation thinks it's so modern, that your ideas are new, that what you suffer is new. It's as old as time. Modern families. Chosen families. Logical families," she said dismissively. "What nonsense. It's family, plain and simple, and you do what needs to be done." Mrs. Green replaced the cap onto the mascara wand.

Cordelia looked at her mother's composure, terrified of it.

"Well," she said to her, "you'd know all about that."

"Cordelia, really. I cannot keep having this conversation with you. It is not your concern. I would never have told you had I realised you lacked the wherewithal to handle it."

She zipped up her bag, signalling it was time to return.

"It's funny. Even as a child, you were uncomfortable with secrets. You were always giving yourself away!" The thought still amused her. She could still picture some of Cordelia's predicaments, and her self-imposed priggishness.

"I appreciate the situation was not of your making, at least at first," said Cordelia.

"Well then. Why should my life, or your life, for that matter, why should any of our lives suffer because of a woman who— took advantage of your father's needs. Anyway, Igor has turned out just fine. Such a charming young man. Your father's eyes, of course."

"He shouldn't have been anywhere near the house," Cordelia remonstrated.

"Well, what's done is done."

"It's almost like you wanted him to find out."

"Well, he didn't, and I won't apologise for being curious, and I will not allow you to make me feel bad because of it."

"Doesn't he deserve to know the truth?"

Mrs. Green gathered her belongings and shook herself down, intent on not missing the ceremony. "Perhaps we must content ourselves with a version of the truth that works."

Tristan was transfixed by what had occurred, but it was the collapse of even the pretence of dignified composure which preoccupied him most. It was so marked a departure from all that he understood Cordelia to be, and from the role which she had required of him when their situations were reversed. In her despair, he saw a glimmer of a past self.

He rarely thought of Seb, and yet still he did, sometimes. We move on, but the decay of the past is always there.

And he saw in Freddie a pattern of behaviour he had failed to know in Seb. Seeking out parallels had become an annoying force of habit, heaving the same old anchor overboard, long after the ship had set itself free. Freddie was a grown man; Seb a little boy, really, offering all that he could of himself, and the detail of him—all the things which made him *him*—that had faded long ago, and now all Tristan could see was the discarded fragments, the shards his memory refused to leave behind.

"People make mistakes," said Dominick, lightly, noting the glistening formation of a cold sore on Tristan's lip, readying itself to star in the photos. They were standing on the first-floor balcony, looking down onto the Grand Hall.

"Freddie doesn't think it's a mistake."

"No, I guess not. But it is not our concern."

"It is, though," Tristan replied.

The hardness of his judgments, his holding people to these standards, his good opinion, once lost, lost forever; such unattractive qualities, yet still he persisted with them.

"It concerns us because I am concerned by it."

Dominick exercised patience, accustomed to Tristan's perplexities. "You've got to—let people live their lives." Two of their guests walked towards them, looking for their room on the

182

second floor. "They'll do it anyway, with or without your blessing."

"Is he still here?" Tristan asked after they passed. "Freddie, I mean."

"He's still here."

"Good."

"You should tell him that," said Dominick.

"He should count himself lucky he was invited at all."

It was a complex anger. Tristan was in awe of Freddie's self-assurance, of his unwavering commitment to his own wants and needs, but a life predicated on wants and needs alone, surely Freddie knew those were the shakiest of all the foundations? Tristan disapproved of the blitheness with which Freddie was condemning Cordelia to a life without him, and worse, to a life whose architecture was Freddie's still. He was affronted by its callousness: on its own terms, but also because it made clear just how little Freddie ever understood of Tristan's own suffering, of the extent to which *he* had been flattened by grief. Freddie slithering out of his marriage, his indifference to it, the absence of value he placed on it, wanting simply to be free of it, it made Tristan afraid. Might he one day feel like that? Might Dominick?

He thought of all his early efforts to shackle Dominick to him, tying him into holidays and plans, knowing the fragility of even the most solemn bonds.

"I'm not saying it will be different for us," said Dominick. "No one can give you that guarantee, but maybe it will be different, maybe we won't mess it up. It's possible. And it's worth the risk. You are worth the risk."

How Tristan had ever persuaded this man to share his life with him! It was the achievement of his life.

*

In the next-door room, Cordelia paced around in a circle, repeating the first line over and over. "'*Let me not to the marriage of two minds admit impediments.*'"

She asked Igor for the next line and then the one after that. He advised lifting her tone at the end of every line before '*O no!*'.

"Like this," he said, demonstrating his point quite well.

She took it from the top and made it to the fifth line before he stopped her again.

"It's 'ever fix—*ed*'! You have to say the 'ed'. 'Fix—*ed*'!"

Cordelia peeked round the door into the Grand Hall to observe the people filing into the library. They had a couple more minutes.

She tried again and Igor looked on approvingly as she nailed "*Love's not Time's fool*" the way he told her, breathing from her diaphragm, speaking melodically, starting high, ending low.

"'*Love alters not with his brief hours and weeks,*'" she continued, "'*but bears it out, even to the edge of doom.*'"

*

"I dreamt of Toby last night," Dominick told him. "The first time in a long time. It's like I want his permission to marry you. Or his forgiveness, maybe."

It felt wrong, all these ghosts visiting upon them, the most painful of the dialogues between soul and self. And Toby's death was so shocking still: all that he knew lost, his loveliness long since faded from the world. He was so much more than they ever knew him to be.

"I doubt Toby expected either of us to sacrifice our lives just because he no longer valued his," Tristan replied, unsure that was true. He felt guilty about his happiness; sometimes, he thought of Dominick as a luxury acquired at Toby's expense.

184

"Come with me," Dominick said, taking Tristan's hand, and walked him towards their room.

He closed the door, turned to face him.

"I don't want to erase him from our past."

He reached into the drawer of a side cabinet for an envelope with Toby's name on it. Tristan took it from his hand.

"What is it?"

"Open it."

Tristan slid the single sheet of paper out of its envelope. It was handwritten, the ink faded, the paper now yellow. Tristan recognised Seb's handwriting and he recognised the ink from the pen he had used to write it. The pen was a gift; it was the first of Seb's birthdays they had celebrated together. He took a deep breath and started to read.

> *A spark, ignited by chance,*
> *radiating an energy I once knew,*
> *defiant.*
> *I carry the feeling of you.*
> *It grows and it grows, and*
> *it has my control.*
> *Why must we abandon*
> *the shape of our dreams*
> *when our dreams are all we know?*
> *It is fire and*
> *the path is scorched, but*
> *everything I see is the colour of life.*

Tristan refolded the paper, lodged it back into the envelope and returned the thing to Dominick, his hands shaking.

So now he knew.

"I've read this before," he told Dominick. "There were drafts of it in my apartment." Tristan remembered working his way through the boxes Seb left behind, looking for clues, and he remembered the shock of his discovery, the sordidness of it. He could still summon that feeling.

"Have you read it?" he asked Dominick.

"There was a time when it was all I could read."

Tristan took another deep breath.

"When did you even find it?"

"Not that long after he died."

"Jesus."

"It was a blessing, actually. It helped set me free." Dominick saw Tristan's disbelief. "Really."

"You should have shown it to me. You should have shown it to me at the time."

"I didn't want you to think less of him."

"You have carried the weight of this around with you, alone, for all this time? You didn't have to do that."

"I did it out of love for you."

*

Cordelia kept her head down as she and the children fought their way to the seats Igor had reserved for them. She guided the children into the row and seated herself nearest the aisle, readjusting her fastener to shield more of her face. She looked around and noticed Freddie slinking in, selecting a seat at the back. Most of the other faces she didn't recognise, although she assumed they now knew her.

When did all these people enter Tristan's life? When did that happen? Is this what he was building when she looked away?

She relegated the thought to her mind's hinterland. There was comfort in the noise of the children chattering about whatever caught their interest, happily co-existing.

"Hello stranger."

Cordelia recognised the voice, its exuberance.

She turned to her left. "Camilla!" She felt something close to cheer, or possibly relief. Camilla looked joyous, radiant in plum, a sequinned boatneck with a waterfall tier.

"What are you doing here?" Cordelia asked her.

"I'm Igor's plus one."

"He didn't mention bringing anyone. I didn't know you even knew each other."

"Everyone knows Igor."

"Seemingly."

"We were at university together," she added.

Camilla was seated at the end of the row, up against a wall, cocooned by the other guests gathering around and jostling for the remaining seats. Camilla introduced herself to the children, full of barely contained excitement, and the children responded in kind. Camilla had always been like this, Cordelia remembered, her mood infectious. But there was something about the way she engaged with the children which made Cordelia think she didn't have her own, and she wondered if that was by accident or design.

They were interrupted by the celebrant's announcement inviting guests to enjoy the ceremony without social media. Tristan, these days professionally hardened, didn't want the YouTubers in the audience using his wedding footage as content.

Cordelia reached into her bag and turned off her phone. It was new and came with a new number. It had been suggested to her she do this so she could stop expecting Freddie's call.

He'd never tried to call her, not once, still hadn't, but at least now she didn't know that for certain.

Igor waved at them from the front of the room.

"Did you not want to sit with him?" she asked Camilla.

"Oh no. It wasn't even suggested. He has his duties to perform. Unofficially, of course." Tristan's best man should have been Toby, and he didn't have the heart not to let him have it, even in death.

"He told you about that?"

Camilla nodded.

"Did he tell you why?"

"He did. I was so sorry to hear that news."

Cordelia rubbed at the pain in her right hand.

"You're not about to hit someone again, are you?"

"God. You saw that? I'm so sorry you saw that."

"I have no doubt at all he deserved it."

"He's not even sorry."

"They usually aren't."

Cordelia reached for a tissue. "You're not seeing me at my best."

"At your best, at your worst—I'm just glad to see you."

Cordelia smiled and swapped seats with her son so she and Camilla could say things the children couldn't hear.

"Anyway," said Camilla, "what we think are the worst of times often turn out not to be." She angled herself towards Cordelia's left ear. "Being angry doesn't make you an angry person. He deserves your anger, and you are entitled to it. Let me tell you a secret. I buy crockery from second-hand stores just so I can smash it up with a rolling pin."

"You do not!"

"I do."

There was a second of silence, but they couldn't contain it. It crept out as a suppressed giggle, quickly grew past the point of no return; they were head in hands besides themselves with laughter, and when they caught each other's eye, they were completely overcome, gasping for air, wiping the tears running down their cheeks.

*

The celebrant knocked on the door, told him it was time. Leaving the sanctuary of this room and making his way to the ceremony, it was immensely onerous to contemplate, and he was afraid.

To know what you have, you must also know its opposite, and to know who you are, you must know whom else you might have been.

The value Tristan placed on Dominick, the esteem in which he held him, it was because of who he was, but also because of who he was not. Tristan wished he could offer Dominick a more innocent love, one which knows no hazardry, but it had been wasted on another, as it always is, and now was lost.

"I want to marry all of you," Dominick told him once, when they were fighting. "I don't want the love you gave others. I want the love of the man you are now, in all its complexity. I want all its wounds, all its ecstasies. I want all of it."

Tristan located his cufflinks, inserted his collarbones, and brushed the cat hair off his jacket.

How easy our lives would be if we were our achievements.

Could they realistically commit to making each other happy for the rest of their lives, in a world which never changes but which is nonetheless full of change? If they tore it all down, would either of them have it in him to start over?

Tristan walked through the hallways, watched by the eyes in the framed portraits lining the walls.

He knew what it was to live the wrong life, a life which did not justify the suffering required to sustain it. And now he knew that, out of the wound, comes salvation.

He stopped outside the doorway which led to the library where the ceremony would take place.

All the change in his life, its beginnings and its endings, the people he had lost along the way. It was a skill, knowing how to dislocate himself from an ideal, learning how to set himself free, letting go to make space for all that is yet to come.

When he opened the door, he could feel the eyes of the people on his left and of those on his right; he feared losing his composure, for the first time he understood the meaning of a white-knuckle ride. He willed on his shaking legs.

For his life to look like this, for any of it even to be possible. To be alive for it, to be alive to it.

He thought about what people do for each other, and to each other, our transgressions and betrayals, our flaws and our infatuations, the improbabilities of who we are, and the hurt we cause ourselves, even when trying to do what is right.

He took his place, touched Dominick's arm, opened his mind to the expansiveness of the moment. He so wanted to believe it would never end, that it was for life.

He placed his hands in his and when he looked up, their eyes met and everything he could see was his future.